"Fasten your seat belt for another marvelously divine encounter with the Perfect Stranger! Once again, Gregory masterfully demonstrates just how passionately and intimately our God loves each one of us. If you are looking for an encouraging faith encounter, the *Perfect Stranger* books are the most palatable and powerful tools of our day."

—SHANNON ETHRIDGE, best-selling author of *Completely His, Every Woman's Battle,* and *Every Woman's Marriage*

"While I liked *Dinner with a Perfect Stranger* very much, I loved *A Day with a Perfect Stranger.* This book has the potential to make people think about what drives them, what keeps them from God, and what will ultimately fulfill them. In a feelings-based and satisfaction-driven society, this is an invaluable tool. People are hungering for the answers to questions Mattie gets to ask. I can't wait to hand it out to friends who do not yet know the Stranger in their midst."

—LISA T. BERGREN, best-selling author of *The Begotten*

"Deftly using narrative to touch on common objections to belief in God, [Gregory] contrasts religiosity with relationship with God. As a light, brief introduction to the faith, *A Day with a Perfect Stranger* is a good pick for women seekers."

—*Aspiring Retail*

# The
# Next Level

A Parable of Finding Your Place in Life

# David Gregory

WATERBROOK
PRESS

THE NEXT LEVEL
PUBLISHED BY WATERBROOK PRESS
12265 Oracle Boulevard, Suite 200
Colorado Springs, Colorado 80921
*A division of Random House Inc.*

ISBN 978-1-4000-7243-9

Library of Congress Cataloging-in-Publication Data
Gregory, David, 1959-
   The next level : a parable of finding your place in life / David Gregory. —
1st ed.
        p. cm.
   ISBN 978-1-4000-7243-9
   1. Self-actualization (Psychology)—Fiction. I. Title.
   PS3607.R4884N49 2008
   813'.6—dc22

                                    2007034314

Printed in the United States of America
2008—First Edition

10 9 8 7 6 5 4 3 2 1

*To my mentor,*

*Sandra Glahn*

# 1

LOOKING FOR A JOB was the last thing Logan Bell wanted to be doing that morning. Playing video games, hiking, body-surfing, sleeping in—he could think of a hundred preferable alternatives. But none paid the bills, and none provided an answer the next time his dad called and said, "So, Son, found another job yet?" That, perhaps, was his greatest motivation: having an answer. Any answer.

His dad, he had to admit, was right. Walking out on his first job after college, even if the boss was a complete jerk, didn't look good on Logan's résumé. Better to get another job immediately than take a much-needed break—especially a job at a leading software company. Logan's undergraduate business degree might never land him where his dad was, near the top of a major high-tech company. But working for one would count for something. Or so Logan thought as he pulled into the massive parking lot of Universal Systems Inc.

"I'm here to apply for a job," Logan told the first-floor receptionist.

She smiled and pointed to a bank of elevators on her left. "You need to see the Director. Fifth floor."

"Is it true that you have to apply here in person?"

"Yes. You need to see the Director. Fifth floor."

"The Director? Director of what—human resources?"

"No, the Director of the company."

"You mean the CEO? The CEO sees people who just walk in off the street?"

"Yes."

"Is there someone a little lower down I could talk to? I'm not looking for an upper-level job."

"No. The Director personally interviews all job candidates."

Logan couldn't imagine how the CEO of an organization so large could interview all applicants. Universal Systems occupied the entirety of an immense circular building with five unusually tall stories. Behind the receptionist, in all directions, stretched the first floor as far as the eye could see. It was filled with employees sitting at desks and in cubicles.

There seemed to be no point, however, in further discussing whom he should talk to. He stepped toward the elevators, then turned back to the receptionist.

"Where do I go once I get to the fifth floor?"

"You go to the Director's desk."

"And where would that be?" Based on what he saw on the first floor, he could imagine wandering for hours trying to find the Director's desk.

"You won't have any trouble finding it," she assured him.

He turned and walked toward the elevators, unsure how her answer could possibly be true.

A few moments later the elevator doors opened to another expanse. Like the first floor, the fifth extended as far as the eye could see. There were no walls to impede one's view of its massive length and breadth, just desks stretching forever. In fact, unlike the first floor, this one was almost bereft of people. In the distance, a group sat around a conference table. Beyond them, Logan noticed a man sitting at a desk. He walked in that direction.

The man behind the leather-topped oval desk looked to be about forty. He was dressed in a brown business suit with a blue tie. The nameplate on the desk read simply "Director." He rose from his chair and extended his hand.

"Welcome to the fifth floor. What can I do for you?"

"My name is Logan Bell. I came to apply for a job."

"Wonderful. Have a seat."

Logan sat in a leather captain's chair in front of the desk. "I'm...I'm a bit surprised to be directed to you. Do you really interview all applicants?"

"Yes, of course."

"Do you have any openings? I've heard that this is *the* place to work."

"We always have openings."

"I'd like to see if I'm a match for any of them."

"You will be."

"What do you mean? You don't know what I do."

"All our job classifications are always open," the Director replied.

This had quickly become the strangest interview Logan had ever experienced. Not that his experience was that extensive: a couple of summer jobs in high school, one all four summers of college, and his first postcollege position.

"You mean, you are always hiring for *all* jobs?"

"Yes."

"Universal Systems must be growing by leaps and bounds." The second Logan said it, he cringed. That sounded so...juvenile, and it betrayed the fact that he hadn't bothered to do a lick of research on the company before arriving.

The Director, however, didn't seem to react adversely. "Yes, we are always growing." He leaned back slightly in his chair. "So what is it you would like to do, Logan?"

"Well..." Logan couldn't believe he was being asked such an open-ended question in an interview—assuming this really was a legitimate interview. "My degree is in business management. In my first job out of school, I was a human resources generalist at a chemical plant. But I'd like to work for a company like yours. My father is a senior vice president at Vescon Technologies, so...I figure high-tech is a good direction."

"Why don't you go to work there?"

"I just don't know if that would work out so great, long term."

"I understand."

"So do you have any HR jobs available?"

"Of course," the Director replied. "But let me ask you a question. Did you enjoy human resources?"

"Well, I realize my first job was entry level, and I would naturally be advancing into positions that would be more..." He stopped. It was all BS, he knew. And something about this place and this man told him he could drop the BS. "No, not really."

"Then there's no point in having you do that, is there? What do you enjoy doing?"

Most of what he enjoyed doing, Logan figured, would be of little use to a company. But within his field of study, he found one topic especially interesting. "I really like OD—that's organizational development." He hesitated. "I suppose you know that. Anyway, I like to examine how a group or an organization works and figure out ways it can work better."

"Then let's have you be an organizational analyst. We've needed someone to do that kind of assessment here for some time. You sound like just the man."

"Are you sure? I mean, I don't have any real background in that. I just liked it best in school."

"That's good enough. You'll learn more on the job."

"Do you want to see my résumé?"

"No," the Director replied. "You strike me as a bright, capable young man. I'm sure the quality of your work is fine."

"Should I bring it for my second interview?"

"There is no second interview. You're hired."

"Just like that?"

"Just like that. I always trust my first instinct."

Logan stared at him, dumbfounded.

The Director leaned forward in his chair. "Do you wish to accept the job or not?"

"Yes. Absolutely. I mean…I just can't believe…" He shut up while he was ahead.

"So," the Director continued, "let me further explain your job to you."

Logan was to start on the first floor. An HR person named Kyle would set him up. He was to assess operations on that level—talk to employees, attend meetings, observe processes. Kyle would arrange access to everything he needed. He was to determine the biggest problem on the floor and report back to the Director.

"Wouldn't it make more sense to assess the organization as a whole rather than level by level?" Logan asked.

"In most organizations that would be the case, but in this one the various levels operate independently. Each division of the company occupies a separate floor. They don't have much interaction."

"Maybe that's a problem."

The Director smiled. "Yes, I've considered that."

He wrote something on a Post-it note and handed it to Logan. "You can simply e-mail me. Nothing long and complicated. Just your basic observations. You don't have to impress me with your report-writing ability."

It all sounded simple. His job was to hang out, see how things worked, and determine what the problems were. Nothing could be easier. If he had written a dream job description himself, it wouldn't have been this good.

"Do you have any questions?"

He hated to interject anything uncomfortable into the discussion, but certain issues hadn't been addressed.

"You haven't mentioned salary…"

"I'll let Kyle go over that with you. I'm confident you'll find the pay acceptable."

"And benefits?"

"Ours are top notch. Kyle will review them with you."

"And who will be my supervisor?"

"You'll report directly to me."

"To you? Always?"

"Yes. You'll be my right-hand man, so to speak. My eyes and ears in the organization."

"What would be my opportunities for advancement? That's pretty important to me."

"I understand. If you successfully analyze each of the first four levels, you will have the option of joining me here on the fifth. If you do"—he nodded toward those at the conference table—"you will be in pretty exclusive company. You will be rewarded commensurately, of course. But first you must succeed at your assignment."

"So all I need to do is tell you the biggest problem on each level."

The Director nodded. "Correct. Things around here are pretty simple, aren't they? But don't expect it to be easy." He stood and extended his hand across the desk. "I am pleased to have you with us."

Logan shook it. "Thank you, sir. I hope I can live up to the trust you've placed in me."

"Come back and talk to me anytime," the Director replied. "Tell me how things are going. If you have any questions or concerns, feel free to come up."

"Who should I contact to set up an appointment?"

"No one. Just come up to the fifth floor."

"Your secretary doesn't screen people?"

"I don't have a secretary. Just drop in. I'll be here."

"Okay…thanks. I mean, thank you, sir."

Logan turned around, hiked past the conference table to the elevators, and descended to the first floor. He didn't have the nerve to ask what he was really wondering—why the Director had the entire fifth floor virtually to himself. It seemed an awful waste of space, a problem he might note at a later date. But that wasn't his concern at the moment. He was just glad to have a job—and a better one than he had ever imagined.

# 2

AFTER TWENTY MINUTES OF WALKING past various color-coded sections of Level One, Logan finally arrived at the desk of his HR contact, Kyle Reidmeier. A thin young man who looked as if he had just stepped out of *GQ*, Kyle stood as Logan approached. Logan introduced himself.

"The receptionist told me I was supposed to select a desk anywhere on the floor."

"That's true. It's up to you. Which area appeals to you?"

"How do employees work anywhere they want to?"

"We can teleconference with anyone in the whole complex."

"Do you ever get together as a group?"

"The HR crew meets once a week for lunch, plus we have our weekly staff meeting. The first floorers, that is."

"What about the people on the other floors?"

Kyle looked at him as if he were crazy. "We don't intermingle with them."

"Oh. I see. Well, I guess it doesn't matter where I sit. I usually like sitting close to those on my work team…"

"Since you're the only OD guy down here, there's not much of a team for you to sit with. I'd be happy to have you here near me. Most everyone else around here is a techie, and it would be nice to have someone nearby who speaks normal English."

"Sounds great." Logan plopped his backpack on a nearby work station and sat down in the chair opposite Kyle's desk. They discussed his pay (which was more than adequate, as the Director had indicated), benefits (impressive as well), and various Level One procedures, of which there were thankfully few. Kyle concluded by saying, "I thought I might show you around—introduce you to some of my team members. You're not exactly HR, but you're close enough that we might let you into the club." He smiled as they rose and started their tour.

"You'll never find success working at this place." Kyle and Logan stood across a desk from Phil Lynch, a slightly overweight man in an out-of-style striped shirt. "But since you're here, have a seat."

They sat in two chairs facing Phil's desk, the same configuration that all the work stations had.

"I forgot to tell you," Kyle said, "Phil's the optimist of the group."

"I'm just being realistic," Phil countered. "Admit it, Kyle."

Rather than being put off by Phil's blunt manner, Logan was actually drawn in by the conversation. He wanted to find out all the dirt on the company that he could. Better to learn it now, before he had wasted six months or a year.

"What do you mean, I'll never find success here?"

"They don't pay you enough."

"It seems pretty good to me."

"Sure, for a worker bee. But how are you going to get rich working for someone else, doing HR?"

"OD," Kyle corrected.

"Who said I'm looking to get rich?" Logan asked.

"If you aren't, you're a fool. That's what it's all about. Show me someone who's fulfilled in life, and I'll show you a fat bank account, a vacation home on the coast, and at least one foreign sports car parked in the garage just for the fun of it."

"Tell him about your plan to get rich, Phil."

"Fifty-eight percent of the time the New York Stock Exchange goes up the first thirty minutes of the trading day. Here, look." He rotated his computer monitor toward Logan. "Here's what the New York Stock Exchange Composite Index has done in the first thirty minutes for the past ten days. What do you think?"

"Interesting," was all Logan could think to say.

"I'm getting my stockbroker's license, and I'm going to buy and sell only in the first half hour."

"And then what?" Logan inquired.

"And then I'll retire to my own little island in the Caribbean."

"And what would one do down there?"

"Drink mai tais all day. Sit on the beach and look at the girls. Or the guys, in Kyle's case." Phil winked at Logan, who didn't respond. "All I know is, I'll be retired and living the good life."

"Well, I wish you success," Logan concluded. "Good to meet you. I look forward to working together."

"Yeah, right." Phil turned back to his computer. "Hopefully not for too long."

Kyle shook his head as they stepped away. "Don't book your flight to visit Phil in the Caribbean just yet," he advised.

"I wasn't planning on it. Not exactly politically correct, is he?"

"I've had to take my share of Phil's bull."

"Why don't you do something about it? You are HR, after all."

"You know, I just don't think he's worth it. Most people down here are cool with me. You seem to be."

"I am. My brother's gay."

Kyle introduced Logan to several more co-workers who, thankfully, seemed normal enough, at least on the surface. As they walked, Kyle filled Logan in on some of the behind-the-scenes scoop.

"This place is like a soap opera," Logan finally commented.

"You might say that. Wait till you meet the last person."

"Who's that?"

"Beth is her name. She's out today. I'll let you find out more on your own."

They headed to Logan's desk. Before taking his seat, Logan turned to face Kyle. "Hey, I really appreciate you taking time to show me the ropes. This place would be kind of overwhelming without someone doing that."

"No problem. Glad to do it. By the way, I've already scheduled some meetings for you with marketing, sales, software development, and tech support. I put the schedule on your desk."

"Cool. That's great of you to do that for me."

"Sure."

"I was wondering, you want to meet sometime for lunch?"

"Yeah. Friday will work. I'll meet you at our level's cafeteria. It's cheap. Or you can bring a sack lunch. We have employee refrigerators, you know."

"Thanks. I'd always rather buy than cook."

The next morning Kyle escorted Logan to the workspace of the only HR person he had yet to meet: Beth, a tanned woman in her midtwenties with auburn hair and a low-cut black blouse that showed plenty of cleavage when she leaned forward. Which she did as she stuck out her hand across her desk toward Logan.

"Hi. Beth Glaston. Good to meet you."

"You too." Logan tried to avoid staring as he shook hands. "Uh, I missed you in yesterday's tour."

"Oh. Yes. Late night, if you know what I mean. I took a comp day to recover."

He noticed a silver stud in her tongue as she spoke.

The three of them small-talked for few minutes until Kyle pulled Logan away. "She's quite a handful," Kyle commented when they were out of range.

"I can tell." Logan glanced back in her direction, but her head had disappeared behind her computer.

"Let me warn you: she'll come on a little strong."

"Why would I need a warning about that? I wouldn't mind getting to know her better."

"Let's just say that she gets to 'know better' virtually every guy who passes through here. You'd be the latest in a very long line. Not that I speak from experience, of course."

Logan laughed. "All right. I'll have to think about that one. Thanks for the heads-up."

That afternoon Logan was sitting at his desk trying to figure out the internal communication system when Beth leaned over his desk.

"Need any help?" she asked.

Logan gazed up at her. "I've got most of it down, I think. I'm still not sure how to do this conference calling, though."

"The instruction sheet on that is impossible. Here, let me show you."

She pulled a chair around to his side of the computer, brushing her chest against his shoulder as she sat. Logan couldn't help noticing the perfume she was wearing, the form-fitting pink sweater barely concealing her black bra, and the effect she was having on him.

She walked him through the steps necessary to initiate and respond to conference calls.

"That wasn't too bad," Logan commented as they wrapped up.

"You're a quick study. Speaking of which, I'm taking a class at the community college—an art history class."

"Really? I always wanted to take art history but could never fit it in."

"I have a test tomorrow, and I need to finish some memory work on artists and their paintings. Would you be interested in helping me out with that tonight? If you don't have any plans, that is."

"Like, you were thinking…"

"I was thinking about meeting over at my place. Maybe around seven thirty? I'll even throw in some Chinese takeout."

Logan leaned over and pulled up his e-mail on his computer. "You know, Beth…" He hesitated, considering whether he should pass up this opportunity. "I think maybe I'd better get my feet a little wet here before I start hanging out with my co-workers. I do appreciate the invitation, though."

She stiffened a bit in her chair. "Oh. Well, I didn't mean anything by it. I just thought maybe you could help me on my test."

"Sure, I understand. That's cool. Maybe next time."

## 3

THE NEXT WEEK LOGAN had meetings with several Level One managers. Their conversations focused on interdepartmental communication, competition among various functions for resources, unity of vision among departments, the levels at which goal setting occurred, and the amount of employee buy-in to the goals of the division.

Logan was surprised to learn that one manager had his own business that he appeared to run from his desk. "Here, let me show you the orders that came in this morning," he said to Logan, showing him the page from his Web site.

Another manager was on the phone talking about some sort of campaign strategy when Logan arrived. He was, it turned out, running for a city-council seat in the upcoming election.

Two weeks into his assignment Logan had attended enough meetings, conducted enough interviews, and observed enough to have a diagnosis ready for the Director. Utilizing some of his college business textbooks to help with the jargon, he put together what seemed like an impressive analysis. He kept it short, since that's what the Director had said he wanted. He pasted it into an e-mail and pressed Send.

Director:

From a business-systems standpoint, the main obstacle to an efficient operation across all of Level One is the absence of cooperative communication between departments. This is happening both at the supervisory and individual contributor level. This condition arises, I believe, from an absence of mutual sharing of pan-organizational objectives, which creates a tendency for separate operational entities to subvert the strategies of the organization at large in favor of their own departmental agendas. From my observations, this problem is systemic and its relief is unlikely to be predicated upon merely enhanced interdepartmental communication techniques or simplistic management-by-objectives solutions.

My recommendation would be a system-wide re-integration of organizational vision within the matrix of operational objectives. This would necessitate a long-term reorientation of the employee population to the strategic goals of Universal Systems, which would engender greater opportunity for inter- and intradepartmental facilitation of efforts that would be in compliance with the strategic plan of the company.

I would be pleased to discuss with you the next steps of such an organizational imperative.

Regards,
Logan

**In a few minutes Logan received a reply to his e-mail.**

Logan,

Do you mean that people on the first floor aren't working toward the same goals, so they don't communicate honestly with each other, and they tend to undermine each other's efforts?

Director

**Logan pressed Reply.**

Yes, I suppose that's what I'm saying.

**He received an immediate response.**

That's all you needed to say. Good work on your analysis so far. Keep on observing.

"I thought I had that analysis down pat." Logan shook his head and swirled the ice in a cup of Dr Pepper. "I guess I wanted to make an impression by getting it right the first time."

Kyle had a sip of company cafeteria coffee. "Organizational development is tough, man. It's not like an exact science. It sounds like you did have it right. He just wants to be thorough."

"You're right. I should take it as a positive, I suppose."

Logan got up, refilled his cup, and returned with a donut. Kyle looked surprised when Logan handed it to him. "Thanks."

"I saw one on your desk yesterday."

Kyle had a bite. "How did you end up in OD, anyway? Most people don't go to college thinking, 'I want to do OD.'"

Logan laughed. "No, you're right. I wouldn't have even known what organizational development was. I started out as a political science major, which I loved. But my dad, he kind of wore me down on that. By my junior year he convinced me to change to business, which was a lot more practical, he thought. So I endured my two years as a business major. My first job out of school was in HR, actually. The Director and I felt like OD would be a better fit."

"Sounds like your dad got his wish in any case."

"Yeah. I feel like I've been trying to please him my whole life. It's the only thing we have that really connects us, I guess."

Kyle ate his last bite of donut and wiped his mouth with a napkin. "You know, I was listening to a psychiatrist on the radio once. I don't remember anything about the interview except him saying that what everyone is really looking for is the perfect father."

Logan emptied his cup and stood up. "Yeah, well...where are you going to find that? I'm not sure if it's better to have a successful dad or a slacker. Maybe I could find some sluggard who would adopt me and have no expectations for me to live up to."

A week later, after more interviews and meetings, Logan sent another e-mail to the Director.

> My perception is that there is a systemic aversion to risk taking and the promotion of creative, "blue sky" thinking on the first floor. This results both from lack of holistic thinking on the part of managers and the reward of short-term problem solving to the detriment of long-term strategic vision and out-of-the-box innovation. A cultural emphasis on creative vision and the maximization of dis-incentives toward risk-averse behaviors is recommended throughout the operation.

He received an immediate reply.

> Are you saying that everyone down there is playing it safe and we need to encourage them to try new things? Good work again. It seems you've made real progress. Keep on observing.

Three days later, Logan sent another analysis. Two days later, another. The next day, another. The Director's responses were always the same: good work, keep on observing.

"Crap!" Logan looked toward Kyle, who had turned his way. He walked over to Kyle's desk and slumped into a chair. "I don't get it. I just sent another report to the Director, and it's the same answer. I've diagnosed every major problem down here. There's nothing else to report. At this rate I'll never get off this level. No offense."

"None taken. I'd go to another level too if I could find one I wanted to go to. This place is a zoo. Everyone constantly doing their own thing."

"Yeah," Logan replied, suddenly lost in thought about Kyle's last statement. "I know what you mean."

Stopping by later for lunch, Kyle found Logan leaning back in his chair, reading a book, his stocking feet propped up on his desk.

"Well, you've gotten comfortable. What are you reading?"

"Covey's *Seven Habits of Highly Defective People.*"

"I think that's *Effective.*"

Logan put the book on his desk and tossed a tennis ball in the air, catching it on its flight down. "Shall we make this a farewell lunch today?"

Kyle caught the ball on an errant flight. "Why? What's up?"

"I have a new hypothesis on the problem. I'm going to test it this afternoon."

After lunch Logan started dropping by random employees' work stations to see what they were doing. He stopped first at the desk of a young Hispanic woman whose nameplate read "Maria Garcia."

"Hi, I'm Logan Bell, the new organizational development analyst. Do you mind if I ask you a quick question?"

Maria smiled at him. "An organizational development analyst. I didn't know we had any of those."

"Well, you didn't use to."

"Great to have you, then. Go ahead—what can I answer for you?"

"I just want to know what you're working on. I don't mean the project you're on. I mean what you were doing just now."

"My work group is having an appreciation party for our senior member. I was looking for an Italian restaurant for the event."

"That sounds nice. I hope you have a great party. Thanks."

"You're welcome."

He walked another fifty feet and stopped at the desk of Bret Landis, where he went through the same routine.

"Next month I'm starting my MBA program," Bret responded. "I was looking online to see if there is advance reading for any of my classes."

At Logan's next stop Amy Mandell was e-mailing her maid of honor with a wedding-etiquette question. Fifty feet on, Vern Johnson was reviewing the profile of his retirement investments. Melissa Crump was paying bills and balancing her bank account online.

Logan had to wait for Tiara Jackson to get off the phone. He discovered that she was talking with her daughter's day-care supervisor. Sydney Lindon was developing slogans for her son's high school student-council election. Tom Hutchins was reading an editorial on the *Wall Street Journal* Web site. Adela Sanchez was finishing a chick-lit novel. Jared Engerson was checking on his fantasy football team. Timothy Walls motioned for Logan to wait while he finished a video game; he was besting his own high score.

Logan walked back to his desk. He pulled up his e-mail and typed a new message for the Director.

> I think the main problem down here is that, as far as I can tell, no one is ever doing anything related to the goals of the company.

Fifteen seconds later he got a reply.

> Congratulations. I think you've got it. Come up and see me.

# 4

LOGAN PRESSED THE 5 BUTTON on the elevator. When the elevator stopped, he got off, looked around the cavernous floor, and walked once again toward the Director's desk.

"Hello, Logan. Have a seat."

Logan sat in one of the captain's chairs.

"You did excellent work on the first level—in all your diagnoses."

"But my first five... You weren't looking for that kind of input, it appears."

"You cited some important problems. Not as important as your final one, though."

"Yeah. I mean, yes. I'm kind of confused by it, I guess. Why would you allow everyone on Level One to act that way? Do they actually produce any usable software down there? It doesn't seem they are contributing anything to the company at all."

"No, not really."

"I'm curious, do you have profit and loss statements for each division?"

"Certainly. Would you like to see Level One's?"

The Director reached in his desk, pulled out a file, and handed it to Logan, who glanced over the first page. He had never seen such a bad statement. "Level One suffered a huge loss last year."

"I'm afraid so."

"What about before that?" He flipped through several of the following pages. "They have had a huge loss every year. Why do you let that go on?"

"No one here is forced to do what they don't want to do. It's their choice."

"So if everyone down there wants to goof off all the time…"

"If they choose not to align themselves with the purposes of the organization, they have that freedom. That is the wish of the Shareholder."

"The Shareholder? Who is that?"

"The Shareholder is the owner of the company."

"There is only one?"

"We are a privately held company."

"So the Shareholder doesn't care if Level One loses him tons of money every year?"

"He cares. He simply chooses to give them that freedom. Sometimes people change their minds about how they want to function within the company."

"And then what happens?"

"There are four other levels. Anyone can choose a new one. Which brings us to your next assignment: Level Two. Are you ready for the second floor?"

Logan looked across the vast fifth floor, then back at the Director. "I suppose I am. It's just that I became friends with a good guy down on Level One. I hate to leave him there. They aren't accomplishing anything, and, to be honest, they don't seem all that happy."

The Director leaned back in his chair. "That's what happens when we become self-focused, isn't it? Life loses its meaning. As for your friend, I'm glad you connected so well with someone on Level One. No one is keeping him there but himself. He is free to move to another level anytime he wants to. But no one ever does so until they are ready."

"Yeah. I guess. I just hope he moves on."

"I do too." The Director leaned forward. "So, are you ready for the next level?"

Logan nodded.

"You will find Level Two quite a contrast to Level One."

"In a good way, I hope, for the company's sake."

"I will leave that assessment up to you."

The Director stood and extended his hand. "Oh, I meant to ask you—how are things with your father?"

Logan's face brightened. "Better since I told him about my job here. I think he has hope for me after all."

"I'm glad to hear it. Well, it was good to talk with you again, Logan. I hope your experience on Level Two is a positive one."

"I'm sure it will be, sir."

Logan turned around and started back toward the elevator bay. The real work of the company, he figured, must begin on the second floor.

## 5

"HERE IS OUR Employee Code of Conduct."

Logan reached across the desk and took what felt like a five-pound document from Nadine Platt, a conservatively dressed woman with gray hair pulled back in a bun.

"It is the policy of this division for our employees to exercise good faith, honesty, propriety, and integrity in all their dealings inside and outside the company. The Code of Conduct encapsulates our efforts to ensure that this policy is carried out to the best of our abilities. You are responsible for reading and understanding its contents and affirming in writing that you will abide by it."

Logan balanced the volume in one hand. "Do I have to finish reading it while I am still on Level Two?"

She glared at him.

"Sorry," he said sheepishly. "It just seems kinda big."

"Integrity is important business." She rose from her desk and motioned for him to follow her. "I'll review for you some of our division's rules that you won't find listed in the Code of Conduct." They began walking down a long aisle bordered by desks on both sides. Logan noticed that all employees' work stations were immaculate.

"All company assets are to be employed for division purposes, not for personal use or personal profit. You'll find that in the Code, of course. Personal calls are to be limited to two minutes except in the case of emergencies. Then you may talk for three. Personal use of the Internet and use of personal communication devices are to be limited to ten minutes per day."

They passed a group of copy machines. "We recycle copy paper. Please stamp 'reuse' on paper you are finished with and place the clean side faceup in the recycle bin."

They walked by more desks. "Personal containers of candy or nuts are allowed at work stations. A maximum of four pieces of candy and twelve nuts is permitted."

"Why so few?"

"We don't want to promote unhealthy lifestyles among our employees. Open desks, by the way, must remain no less than ninety-eight inches apart. Measuring tapes may be borrowed from section managers if you need to verify."

"Why ninety-eight inches?"

"To prevent eavesdropping on others' work conversations."

"That's still pretty close."

"You will find ear mufflers in your lower right-hand desk drawer. Please keep them on your desk, and use them when necessary."

They passed a conference room on their left. "We have twelve conference rooms on this level. They must be reserved three days in advance. Section-manager approval is required for groups larger than three. No food or drink is allowed except water and nonsticky candies, like SweeTarts. You can call the Compliance Line if you have questions about a particular candy. Four pieces per person, maximum. Employees are responsible for cleaning the conference rooms after each use. When necessary, conference tables are to be cleaned with Old English brand furniture polish."

"Can't we use Pledge?"

She rolled her eyes. "No, you may not use Pledge."

They went through a pair of glass doors that led into a kitchen. "This is the kitchen area assigned to you. There are five others on this level, but they are off-limits to everyone outside those areas. The kitchens are open from 11:30 a.m. to 1:00 p.m."

"They're not open for breaks?"

"No, they are not. When the kitchens are locked at 1:00 p.m., they must be spick-and-span. No exceptions. Anyone found in violation will lose kitchen privileges for a month."

They exited the kitchen. "The division has a strict dress code, which your attire does not meet. You can look up the dress code in the Employee Code of Conduct. You will have to leave the premises immediately after our discussion and return wearing the appropriate attire. I will escort you to the elevators. You will be docked for half a day of personal time."

"Half a day? I only live twenty minutes from here."

"Half a day. Any employee failing to comply at all times with the dress code will be disciplined. Do you have any questions before we proceed to the elevator and you attend to your attire?"

"No, I think you probably covered it."

What he actually wondered was how people got anything done in this maze of rules and regulations.

Upon his return to the Universal Systems building, Logan raced to a one-on-one meeting with Darrell Stiles, the Level Two General Manager. Logan was ten minutes late.

"I'm so sorry," he said upon entering the GM's office. "I had to go home and change."

The GM laughed as they shook hands. "That's all right. It sounds like Nadine got to you."

"You might say that."

"We could have cut you some slack on your first day, but thanks for accommodating us. Have a seat. So you've already completed your assessment of the first floor?"

"Yes sir. It was…an enlightening experience."

"I imagine you'll find your experience up here a nice contrast. You'll have to take Nadine with a grain of salt, by the way. She means well, but she does go overboard a bit on the regulations."

Logan grinned. "You mean we really can use Pledge on Level Two?"

The GM frowned. "Well, no. We do prefer Old English."

"Oh."

"We don't have a bunch of rules on Level Two just for the sake of having rules. Our real focus is on integrity. We believe that integrity is the highest value an organization or an individual can have. We seek to embody honor and consideration in all our dealings both inside and outside the company."

"Are you the only level that places this kind of emphasis on it?"

"Hmmm. That's hard to say. Levels Three and Four certainly have it as a core value as well. But if I may boast a little, I believe we practice it as a higher priority than anyone else in the company. We find that if you practice the utmost integrity in your dealings with others, then you inevitably treat yourself with integrity. And if you treat yourself with integrity, you will maximally advance the interests of the organization. It's a reinforcing cycle, one that never fails to work. I think you will find all our employees are highly committed to it."

"That sounds great. Maybe this would be a good time to talk about setting up some meetings."

"I've already planned the first step for you. Tomorrow morning at 8:00, I have a strategic planning meeting with all seven of the operating managers who report directly to me. It's our most important meeting of the month. I thought it would give you a taste of how we do things around here."

"Cool. I mean, thanks. I would love to be there."

"Super. I'll show you where the conference room is. As for this afternoon, we'll get you set up at your desk."

The next morning at 7:55 Logan arrived at the designated conference room. All seven of the GM's direct reports were present, and the meeting had already begun. The talking stopped when Logan entered.

"Welcome, Logan." The GM pointed to an empty chair and turned to his managers. "This is Logan Bell, our new organizational development hire."

Everyone nodded at him.

"Logan is assessing operational efficiency on each level of the company. I have given him free rein of the floor, to talk to anyone and sit in on any meeting, disciplinary meetings excluded. I have no doubt about the nature of his report for this level, of course." He chuckled, and several managers knowingly smiled. "I think he'll find everything we do is shipshape."

Logan pulled out his computer notebook. The GM turned to a whiteboard that had a large chart on it with numerous categories listed down one side and weeks listed across the top. "Needless to say, Logan has never seen the chart we use for our primary strategic planning. Logan, you're about to see it in action."

He looked around the table. "Okay. Let's see how we've been doing. How many of you have had employees report potential conflicts of interest to you this past week?"

Two managers enthusiastically raised their hands, and the GM placed a 2 in a box on the chart.

"How many have had reports of clients giving your employees gifts valued at over one hundred dollars?"

One manager raised his hand. The GM recorded it.

"How many have had invitations by clients to inappropriate events or venues?"

Three raised their hands.

"All right. How many have had employees who reported seeing ethical-code violations?"

All seven raised their hands. The GM pumped his fist. "A perfect score. We've had that for five weeks straight now. How many of you have had salespeople admit to fudging on the truth to customers?"

Three raised their hands. "We've got to work on that. We want our sales force to have the reputation as the most honest in the industry." He recorded a 3.

"All right. What about employee use of resources? How many of you discovered inappropriate employee use of the Internet?"

Two managers responded. The GM turned to the first. "What was he or she looking at?"

"Canadian curling scores from two days before."

The GM shook his head, then turned to the other manager. "And yours, June?"

"Looking up a recipe for chicken and jalapeño enchiladas. She was reprimanded."

"Good. Okay, we didn't do too badly there, not out of a thousand employees. Last but not least, what about promptness? How many have had any employees arrive later than 7:45 in the morning?"

One manager reluctantly raised his hand.

The GM shook his head. "Same guy?"

"Yeah."

"What time has he been averaging showing up?"

"Seven fifty-one."

"Okay." The GM paused. "Well, that gives us room for improvement again, which is not necessarily a bad thing. All right, let's turn to our strategic planning."

Logan had not yet used his notebook. He was confident that, having taken care of the minutiae, the group would now get down to the serious business of the division.

The GM handed his dry-erase marker to one of the managers. "I've asked George to lead this next part of the discussion. George has been focusing on this topic area, and I thought he would be best qualified to lead us on it."

The GM sat, and George got up and went to the board. "Thanks, Darrell." He faced the group. "We've talked in here several times about our need to improve performance in the area of employee kitchen cleanliness." The managers all nodded. Logan looked around the table, then typed "Kitchen Cleanliness" on his notebook.

"The division's policies on this matter are clearly laid out in the Code of Conduct, of course. But compliance has become a real issue. We've had clients come in to be pitched by our sales teams, and they pass by our kitchens and see a coffee stain on the Formica or pieces of spinach lasagna left in the sink. I actually witnessed that one myself." There was an audible gasp around the room. "Needless to say, we didn't make the sale.

"Obviously, the performance of the entire division is being jeopardized by this issue. I have some ideas myself, but I'd like us to brainstorm ways we might be able to address it."

Numerous solutions were proposed, from full-time kitchen monitors to using only paper plates and plastic utensils. In the end the group decided to have employees take time off from their regular work for shifts as kitchen monitors. This would both optimize kitchen cleanliness and improve employee character by having all employees take responsibility for the problem.

The meeting broke up, and Logan followed the GM back to his office. "I'm glad you got to be a part of that, Logan. There's nothing quite as thrilling as seeing how a large operation like this does its strategic planning and translates that into here-and-now priorities. I trust you got all the notes you needed?"

"Yes, I think I did."

"Great. Now, how shall we set up the meetings you'll need? You'll have to tell me the kinds of employees you want to interview and observe in action."

Logan hesitated. "You know, I think I'd better get back with you on that. The meeting we were just in has really…caused me…caused me to rethink how I might approach my analysis on Level Two. Do you mind if we revisit this tomorrow morning?"

"No, that would be great. Just e-mail me, and we can set a time."

Logan returned to his desk and e-mailed the Director. He got an immediate reply.

That was quick. Come on up and let's chat.

# 6

"Congratulations on assessing the main problem on Level Two so quickly." The Director put a cup of coffee down on his desk. "Can I offer you something to drink?"

"Do you have a Dr Pepper?"

"I have a Coke."

"That'll be fine."

The Director reached into a minirefrigerator and handed Logan a can. He opened it and took a drink before responding to the Director's statement.

"Level Two wasn't hard to figure out. They're so…well, I don't mean to be rude."

"You can be honest. That's why I hired you."

"They're so tied up in their rules and regulations that they don't have time for anything else. Can I ask you—do they make a profit in that division?"

The Director handed him another folder with profit and loss statements.

Logan looked them over. "Not as bad as Level One, but they haven't made a profit in the last five years. Not even close, really. What about before that?"

"The same."

"Why are they so caught up in rules?"

"They're not primarily focused on rules. They're focused on integrity, just as they probably told you. The rules are simply a manifestation of that. Unfortunately, being people of integrity, or being good, if you will, is their entire focus."

"It seems kind of ridiculous to say this, but…"

"But what?"

"In a sense they're not that different from Level One, are they?"

"Why do you think that?"

"Because basically they're just doing their own thing, in their own way, with their own goals. They look a lot better than Level One—with the integrity stuff and all. But they don't have any time left to accomplish the true goals of the organization."

"You are quite right. They are, in fact, doing their own thing as much as Level One is. They are focused on what they want to achieve, not what the Shareholder wants to achieve. Integrity is a wonderful thing. But it's not the only thing. Not even the primary thing."

Logan nodded. "When you take being good to that extreme, it doesn't even seem like you actually do any good—really help people, I mean. Ultimately, that's what our products are meant to do, isn't it? Help people out?"

"Level Two may be doing more of that than you saw. There's one more person on that floor you should talk to. It might change your assessment somewhat."

Upon returning to Level Two, Logan gave Kyle a call. He spoke quietly so as not to be overheard by anyone sitting ninety-eight inches away. "I'm about to move on to Level Three."

"Level Three? You just got to Level Two."

"I know, but this level didn't take any time at all to diagnose."

"So have you found the ideal level for me?"

"Hardly. I mean, the people up here are mostly nice, and they aren't as messed up as the folks on Level One—well, a little wackier, in a way. Let's just say you'd hate all the regulations."

"When are you moving to Three? I can come help you carry your stuff if you want. Things are kind of slow down here."

"I'll let you know. The Director wants me to talk to one more person first, the Manager of International Operations."

"Cool. Just e-mail me."

Logan was immediately impressed with Cindy Huong, a bright, energetic woman who exuded confidence. She laughed when he described his impression of Level Two.

"Yes, they are a little fixated here. I believe we have avoided that in International Operations. We prefer a much looser approach. The same values—just a different style. We are proudest of the compassion work we are able to do overseas. For example, we have targeted selected spots on the globe and are offering our logistics software at a seventy percent discount. Ninety percent in a few locales."

"Ninety percent? How can you do that? And why?"

"We make up for it with the rest of our operations. As for why, our software is helping local governments and nonprofits manage their resources more efficiently, resulting in better delivery of food, medicine, health services, and so forth to millions in the developing world. We view it as the best way to implement our values as an organization, in addition to the direct charitable contributions we make, of course."

Logan glanced at the latest income statement of her operations. "I'm amazed at how much of your effort goes into this kind of assistance work."

"What exhibits integrity more than helping those without all the advantages we have received in life? Giving back is the least we can do."

"So what did you determine about Level Two's international operations?" The Director reshelved a book he had been reading. Logan sat in a chair across the desk.

"I'm amazed at how much good they are doing. They seem to be actually helping a lot around the world."

"They are, aren't they? Many are benefited."

"To be honest, I can't find any fault in what they're doing. They're not like the domestic Level Two operations at all."

"The two are more similar than you think."

"How?" The statement took Logan aback. "I just don't see it."

"Perhaps you will the longer you keep your eyes open." The Director rose. "Let's leave that an open-ended question. I'll let you sit with it awhile. In the meantime, I've set up your contact on Level Three. I believe you'll find her one of the most pleasant persons you will meet here."

## 7

LOGAN STUCK OUT HIS RIGHT HAND. Rima Bashir, a middle-aged woman with olive skin, took his hand in both of hers. "Welcome to the third floor! It's so very good to have you with us. Have you decided where you want your work station?"

It always unnerved Logan when someone shook hands by taking both of his in hers (it was always a she). At the same time, he kind of liked it. It felt…embracing, as if the person was truly glad to meet him. Rima was that way. She instantly made Logan feel welcomed to the third floor.

They got him settled in at a desk.

"I've been told that you are assessing the strengths and weaknesses of each level."

"Yes. I'm reporting back to the Director."

"This level operates smoothly. We're quite proud of what we accomplish here on Level Three. I think you'll find the perspective here quite different from Levels One and Two."

"How do you mean?"

"You may have noticed that on those levels they don't give a second thought to how the company as a whole operates and what is expected of them from above. On this level, that is very important. It's our broader view that gives our work meaning. I'll let our key managers tell you about that, though. Let me go ahead and introduce you to one of them. He's expecting you."

Rima led Logan to a nondescript, medium-sized office. Inside was a balding man with glasses. He rose and smiled broadly when Rima knocked at the doorway. "Come in, come in! Rima, so very good to see you." He extended his hand toward Logan. "You must be the new organizational development fellow. I'm Saleet. Welcome to Level Three. We're so glad you could join us for a time."

The three of them small-talked for a few minutes before Rima left Logan with the manager. He poured a cup of tea and handed it to Logan. "I hope you like hot tea. Never go a day without it." He poured one for himself and took a sip. "Now, how can I help you in your assessment?"

A Dr Pepper sounded better, but Logan drank some tea to be polite. "I suppose I'm just interested at this point in an overview of your operations. It's my understanding that there are thirteen operations managers in this division, each with substantial autonomy in planning, budgeting, and operations."

"That's correct. We have five major profit centers and eight smaller ones. Mine is one of the five larger ones."

"How does your operation fit into the whole?"

"The General Manager sets very broad direction for the division. Her main job is coordinating the functions of the many different profit centers. We on Level Three pride ourselves in having a much more encompassing vision for the company than do Levels One and Two. Unfortunately—and please don't quote me on this—their viewpoints are rather myopic, and their income statements reflect that, I'm afraid."

"Would you say that all the profit centers on this level have the same vision of the company?"

"Oh no, absolutely not. That's what makes our General Manager's job so difficult, bringing together all these different viewpoints into a coherent scheme. But we do have some commonalities."

"Such as?"

"Unlike Levels One and Two, we appreciate the fact that there is something above us and that we are responsible to report up the ladder. But everyone's take on that is a bit different."

"What is yours?" Logan was typing notes as the manager spoke.

"We believe that there is a true CEO at the head of the company. We've never personally seen him, but we know he is there."

"You mean the Director?"

"No. We all know he is not the real CEO, don't we?"

Logan shifted in his chair. "So…how do you know this other CEO exists?"

"Because a few years back—sixteen, to be exact—a management consultant came to work with our operating group for several months. He said he had heard directly from the CEO, and he had instructions on how we were to conduct our operation."

"How do you know he got instructions from the CEO?"

"The consultant said so."

"What message did he relay, if I may ask?"

"Certainly. He said that everyone who acknowledged the CEO, and him as the CEO's consultant, would be guaranteed a permanent job with us at a great location in the future. Everyone else would one day be fired. In the meantime we are required to do various things."

"Such as?"

"We have to tell everyone about the CEO and the consultant. We have to e-mail the CEO five times a day."

"What do you have to e-mail him about?"

"Whatever we happen to be involved in."

"Does the CEO e-mail you back?"

"No, not that I've heard. We also have to observe silence for half an hour a day."

"What for?"

"To show our devotion to the CEO. We can concentrate better on our work if we're not talking, of course. We have to spend an hour a week helping other employees who need some kind of training. And once a year we have to visit the company's original site, the one before we moved into this building."

"Why is that?"

"Simply honoring our roots, the place where the CEO first revealed himself to us."

Logan shifted the conversation to some of the specific operations overseen by the manager. They discussed control cycles, quality enhancement, and the competitive advantages of the operating group versus its direct competitors. The manager related everything back to the organizational vision that the CEO had provided through the consultant and the rules the entire group had implemented to fulfill that vision. The whole thing, Logan thought, was a bit strange.

He returned to his desk, organized his notes, and processed what he had heard. Who was this CEO? Was it the Director or someone else? Why hadn't anyone ever mentioned this consultant to him? He concluded that he was more likely to get an accurate answer from the Director than from the manager he had spoken to.

Each of the next four days Rima had a meeting scheduled for Logan with one of the other primary operations managers. The interviews all paralleled that with the first manager. Each operation had a certain viewpoint concerning the company. None of the operations seemed to agree on exactly what the company, its leadership, or its purpose consisted of. But they were all convinced of their own view of it, and their activities were governed by their differing views.

The second manager, a smartly dressed man in his early thirties, explained that the true CEO was a former computer programmer who had, through development of both his personal integrity and his management skills, risen to the top of the company. All employees could do the same—would do the same, in fact—if they were dedicated to their purpose. One day all who were dedicated would get to become CEOs of their own spin-off companies.

The third manager, a lively woman in a teal business suit, said that a stream of capitalistic energy and wisdom emanated from the fifth floor. The entire company—the building, the computers, the managers, the employees—were manifestations of that stream. Everyone's job was to get in harmony with it, whereupon unlimited money-making potential would be unleashed.

Employees in her operating group spent a good part of their day "aligning" themselves with this flow. They sat on stacks of business self-help books for twenty minutes at a time and listened to motivational talks on their computers while staring at psychedelic images of thousand dollar bills.

Employees were, she asserted, all CEOs; their biggest problem was they were unaware of their status. One day they would all be aware and enter into capitalistic bliss. "We create our own reality through our keystrokes," the manager claimed. "I can have whatever I want in life. I only have to make sure I strike the right keys and avoid striking the wrong ones."

The fourth manager, a diminutive woman in her fifties, had a view of the company somewhat similar to that of the third manager. She emphasized, however, that all employees were governed by the absolute law of rehire.

"What is that?" Logan asked.

"We all eventually get fired. Then we are all rehired into another position. The position we get hired into depends on how good an employee we were the last time around. This cycle of hiring, firing, and rehiring lasts until we become the perfect employee."

"So what happens when you become the perfect employee?"

"At that point you cease being an individual employee, and you become part of the company as a whole. You are listed on the balance sheet as 'goodwill.' When all of us become goodwill, the company will have achieved ultimate harmony."

The last manager was a tall man with gold wire-rimmed glasses and a goatee. His view, and that of his group, was very specific. "There are four primary truths that we must work by. First, employment by its very nature means suffering. Second, business is ever changing. We suffer because we want to make a profit, which is impermanent. Third, we can be liberated from suffering by eliminating our desire for profit. Fourth, there is a certain path of disciplined work that will eliminate this desire."

"And what happens when the desire is eliminated?"

"We enter a realm in which there is neither business nor non-business, but all is nonprofit bliss."

Logan couldn't imagine that this operating group, given its orientation, was accomplishing much for the company.

After talking to the primary operations managers, Logan was more confused than ever. He considered going up to the fifth level and seeing the Director, but he decided to try to make sense on his own of what he had heard. After all, that's what he had been hired for, to do organizational analysis. He wondered if bouncing some things off Kyle might help.

Logan took the elevator down to the first floor. It looked the same as when Logan left it—lots of people busy accomplishing nothing. He passed by Beth's desk on his way to Kyle's. She looked up and gave a small, expressionless wave. He returned it.

Kyle was sorting through some employee files when Logan approached. "Why do you bother with those?" Logan asked him. "Hardly anyone does any real work down here."

"I don't know. It keeps me busy, I guess. So what's up with your analysis of Level Three?"

"I'm baffled. How can each of the operations centers on that level be accomplishing anything for the company if they can't even agree on what the company is about? They don't agree on who runs it, what its goals are, what the employees are supposed to be doing—nothing. It's as if they all are living in their own little worlds. And none of these little worlds has been mentioned by the Director at all."

"Well, at least they're trying to make sense of this place. Down here we don't give a second thought to any of those things."

"But how can all their stories be so different—and so different from what I see on the fifth floor?"

"I don't know. If employees lose touch with top management, I guess all sorts of conjecture starts floating around. And then people believe it and start organizing their work lives according to it." Kyle picked up a stack of folders and placed them in a drawer. "I take it you're not going to suggest that I move up to the third floor?"

"No, but I have to say this. They have a lot going for them there. Regardless of their view of the company, they seem to be dependable employees—as they define it, at least. There's a lot of talk about being dedicated and loyal and treating others well. It's a pretty good place to work actually—better than Level One. People are generally happier, with one exception, I guess."

"What's that?"

"I don't think the ones expecting to be fired and rehired endlessly are all that crazy about it. It seems pretty hopeless."

"Yeah. You could come back as a tax accountant."

## 8

LOGAN JOURNEYED ONCE AGAIN to the Director's desk. He was uncertain as to what he was going to report.

"I'm not exactly sure how to characterize the main problem on Level Three, but I thought maybe we could talk it through. You said I could come up and talk anytime I wanted."

"Absolutely," the Director replied.

"Is this a convenient time? I just kind of barged in up here." Logan wondered if the Director ever left his desk for anything.

"I'm always available to you."

"Great." Logan retrieved his PDA from his briefcase. "Well, Level Three was certainly different from Levels One and Two."

"How do you think so?"

"Level Three has a greater sense of the whole company, and they're trying to work for that whole."

"Yes, they are."

"And they seem to run a pretty efficient operation overall. I mean, they would be a lot more efficient if they could agree on their aims, but at least within each operating group, they are fairly productive."

"Yes."

"So I guess my question is this: what's the truth about Universal Systems? Each of the different operating groups believes

something entirely different about how the company is consti-
tuted, who leads it, what its vision and goals are, and... I don't
know. It's pretty confusing just talking to the five primary managers. If I talked with all thirteen operating groups, it would be
hopeless."

The Director nodded. "There is quite a wide variety of opin-
ions on that level, isn't there?"

"But everyone seems sincere in their views."

"Oh yes, very sincere."

"One manager I spoke with talked about some consultant
who came through sixteen years ago and carried instructions
from the CEO to Level Three. Another talked about a capitalistic
energy field flowing from Level Five."

The Director chuckled. "I don't know if I would put it in
those terms."

"So what's the real story?"

"The Shareholder is the real owner and Chairman. I am real,
I think." He crossed his arms and patted himself on his shoulders.
"Yes, definitely real. I am the Chief Executive Officer."

"But it doesn't seem like the first three levels take direction
from you."

"They get as much direction as they care to receive. That is
how the Shareholder prefers it."

"So was there a consultant?"

"There was a consultant, but neither the Shareholder nor I
hired or worked with him. That was Level Three's doing."

"So did the Shareholder use to be a computer programmer?"

The Director laughed out loud. "No. He could do that if he wanted to, I suppose—he's quite bright. But, no, he was never a computer programmer."

"Then I don't get it. Why does everyone on Level Three believe all these weird things about the company?"

"Rumors get started in every organization. Sometimes it's easier to believe the rumors than the reality. That's what happened on Level Three."

"Does that division ever show a profit?"

The Director shook his head. "No. About like Level Two, I'm afraid. Not as bad as Level One, but not a profit."

"But I thought they were making a profit. They talk as if they do."

"Yes, well, they have a unique way of accounting down there."

Logan eased back in his chair. "It seems the main problem on Level Three is basically the same as on Levels One and Two. None of them are taking directions from the top, all of them are doing their own thing, and none of them are actually contributing to the goals of the company."

The Director leaned forward. "Very astute. You are completely correct."

"So why don't you and the Shareholder set the employees on Level Three straight? It seems to me that at least some of them would want to know the truth about the company."

"They have that opportunity, which you learn about on Level Four. Are you ready to diagnose your final problem?"

## 9

THE ELEVATOR STOPPED at the fourth floor. The doors opened to a bear of a man with a broad smile and, Logan found out, a strong handshake.

"You must be Logan. Welcome to Level Four. I'm Jack Wilkerson."

The General Manager of the fourth level, Jack Wilkerson had a reputation for somewhat of a cult following among his employees. His business sense was well respected, he was known as an innovator, and he had a dynamic personality to match. Logan immediately noted his skill at making a person feel at home on his level.

"We're thrilled to have you spend some time with us on Level Four. I take it your sojourn on Levels One through Three was enlightening?"

They were already walking down a lengthy aisle, the first leg of what Logan assumed would be a Level Four tour.

"Yes, I suppose it was. I hope my feedback proves valuable to the Director."

Jack smiled. "Oh, I have no doubt about that. The Director can make good use of whatever is presented to him. He excels at that."

They took a right down another aisle. "Let me point out some of the level to you as we talk. I thought I'd give you a tour myself, then we can get you set up at a desk."

"Sounds great."

Logan noticed that each work station had an L-shaped cherry desk with matching bookcase and lateral filing cabinet. Employees certainly had more space and privacy than those on levels below.

"Things on this level are a bit more upscale. Not only the furniture. We have the latest model computers, software, media hookups in the conference rooms, the works."

"Everything does look new. How come?"

"Well, for one, we want the fourth level to be a place employees are attracted to, a winsome place to work. And naturally we want the level to reflect well on both the Director and the Shareholder."

Logan stopped in his tracks. "The Shareholder? You know about the Shareholder?"

Jack laughed. "Of course. How could we possibly carry out his vision for the company unless we knew him personally? And the Director as well, of course. They govern everything we do here."

They continued walking. The GM pointed out a large, enclosed room on the right. "You won't find this on any other level."

"What is it?"

"It's one of our cafés—a coffee bar, really."

Ten or so employees sat around the room, sipping coffee, eating pastries, and chatting or reading. All that was missing was the green Starbucks logo. It was, he had to admit, a nice perk.

"The division provides the drinks, the snacks, and the barista. We encourage staff to spend time here. It's a place where they can read, think, and converse. We have four of them on Level Four."

They walked back toward a conference room on their left. A dozen people sat around the table with a large softbound book in front of each. "Our conference rooms are routinely in use. We encourage employees to get together for both business projects and professional development purposes."

"They look intent on that book."

"That's a Manual review. We have a Manual written by the Director's very first direct reports. It governs everything we do, really. I don't mean the details—just the broad outlines. It sets our vision and reminds us of the heart of the Director and the Shareholder. We encourage employees to spend a lot of time getting to know it. Our whole division prides itself on being as faithful to it as possible."

They came to what looked like the entrance to an auditorium. The General Manager opened two doors, and they stepped inside a state-of-the-art auditorium that looked as if it could seat several thousand.

"Wow." Logan took in the place. "This is pretty impressive."

Jack beamed. "We're quite proud of it. We have something in here every week. We do training sessions, have consultants come speak to our groups, do division briefings, pep rallies—"

"Pep rallies?"

"Well, that's what we call them. They're not corny, like the sales pep rallies you may be thinking of. They're simply occasions when we remind everyone of our common vision and how we are putting that into practice. We have a band that comes in and provides some entertainment—"

"A band? You really do go all out."

"As I said, everything we do is upscale. We want our people to know how important they are to us and also to the Director and the Shareholder."

Logan continued surveying the place as they walked toward the stage.

"We even show movies in here once a month."

"Movies? You're kidding."

"Not at all. They're a great break and a great motivator. The movies we choose have a specific purpose. Afterward everyone breaks up into work units and discusses the implications of the movie for themselves and their work team. People love it."

Logan looked up at the balcony. "It looks like you have way more seating in this place than you have employees on Level Four."

Jack smiled. "Always plan for growth."

"You expect to grow that much?"

"One day most of this company will be on the fourth level. By that time we might have to expand our operations to another level or two. But in any case, most of the people from Levels One, Two, and Three will eventually join us. When they do, we'll have plenty of room for us all in here."

They left the auditorium. Jack handed Logan off to Ben Robinson, an HR generalist with a quick smile.

"I'll set you up with a desk and tell IT to get you going on your computer," Ben said. "There's an open work station right here near me if that suits you. But if you need to be elsewhere on the floor…"

"No, this'll work great."

"So how do you want to get started?"

"I'd like to interact with some of the regular employees. I've been meeting with mostly managers, and I wouldn't mind a different perspective."

"That'll be easy to arrange. I'll take you this afternoon to one of the Manual reviews that we have on the floor. Did Jack mention them?"

"Briefly."

"Throughout the division we have groups of employees that get together once a week to study the Manual. It's a great way to stay focused on the Shareholder's and Director's goals for the company and to see ourselves and our work the way they do. I think you'll enjoy it."

That afternoon Logan sat at a conference room table with a dozen other employees. Everyone had a Manual open in front of them. The group read most of a page. Curt, a software engineering manager, was leading the study. "What are these paragraphs telling us about our work here?"

Logan glanced around the oblong table, but no one spoke. Finally a young woman broke the silence. "Well, it seems to me in these first sentences that, for one thing, the Director doesn't hold it against us when we screw up."

"Good," Curt replied. "How does it feel to know that you're not going to get reprimanded for making a mistake?"

"It feels great," answered a thirtyish man with a shaved head. "It gives us huge freedom to try new things, be innovative, take risks for the sake of the company. And if we mess up, we mess up. No one holds it against us."

Everyone around the table nodded. Logan could tell this was an aspect of the fourth level that really appealed to people.

"So what else do you see?" Curt asked.

The same guy continued. "It's saying that, unlike some levels, we're not strictly regimented. I mean, there are certain things we have to do and not do—we all know that. But there's a lot of freedom within those boundaries."

"It's not like on Level Two," commented a middle-aged woman. "I was on that level for two and a half years. They're keeping rules and trying to be good, as if that were the goal of everything. But it's not. We're trying to fulfill the vision the Shareholder has given us."

"And that's where the middle part of the page comes in," Curt commented. "Who can summarize what's being said here?"

An older gentleman leaned forward. The others leaned in slightly to hear him. "It's saying that we became new employees when we came to the fourth floor. We no longer have to work like we were working before on other levels. The Director enables us to fulfill the purpose for which we were hired."

Curt looked around the table. "Exactly. We aren't the employees we used to be. We've been made new. Why is that?"

A young man answered. "It's because of the sacrifice the Director made for us. When we come to the fourth floor, we become more and more like him."

"Which leads to what?" Curt asked.

Another young woman chimed in. "It leads to our being forever grateful to him and wanting to be productive employees for him in return."

Everyone nodded.

The older gentleman leaned forward again. Logan could see tears in his eyes. "For me, it means this: the Director has become my best friend. He sacrificed for me. Now it's my privilege to sacrifice for him."

"So what is this sacrifice by the Director that everyone is talking about?" Logan sat in a chair across from Ben's desk.

Ben smiled as if he enjoyed answering the question. "Years ago the company was accused of fraud in one of its government contracts. We were charged with significantly overbilling. It was, it turned out, entirely untrue. We were set up by some former disgruntled employees who had worked on Level One. But they set it up pretty good, and it looked like the entire company was going down."

He opened a drawer, flipped through some manila folders, and finally pulled out one. "The Director volunteered to take the fall for it, to get the company off the hook. He was the main one being accused, and he was able to exonerate everyone else while taking the blame himself. The company got a slap on the wrist, while he got prison. He was dragged through the national news."

He handed Logan a copy of a newspaper article with the headline "CEO Found Guilty of Defrauding Government."

Logan glanced over it. "But he must have been reinstated."

"After a couple of years, one of the conspirators admitted framing the Director. The whole conspiracy came to light, and the prosecutor got the Director freed. We look back on that as the defining moment of the company: when the Director sacrificed himself for the good of us all. Until then, most of the company was on Levels One, Two, and Three. After that, this division really started taking off, and the Director gained quite a following. Since then, the fourth level has really dominated the company's activities."

Later that afternoon Logan sent Kyle an e-mail inviting him to lunch on Level Four. They got together the next day.

"You seem all chipper," Kyle commented as they waited for their sandwiches to be grilled. "Found the key problem here so soon?"

"I don't think there is a problem here."

"So what have you found—this level is some kind of corporate nirvana?"

"Not nirvana. Just employees operating at their best, committed to doing their best, and loving what they are doing. I've never seen anything like it, certainly not on the first three levels, not across a whole level like this."

Kyle grabbed his sandwich and a fruit bowl and followed Logan to a small table.

"What makes this division so special?"

"A lot of things." Logan took a bite of his grilled ham and cheese. "I would say the biggest is the tone set by the Shareholder and the Director."

"Who's the Shareholder?"

"He's the owner of the company."

"For real? They know the owner of the company on this level?"

"Yes."

"They get to speak with him?"

"No, but they do study a manual written by the Director's first managers—which, of course, reflects the Shareholder's vision. That's like hearing from him. Another positive is the work environment. They have the best of everything—desks, computers, software, you name it. They are compensated really well. But what's more, the Shareholder promises to take care of them, whatever needs they might have. And beyond that, they are guaranteed a job forever."

Kyle stopped in midbite. "A job forever? You're kidding."

"No. And in the meantime, they get all these sweet perks—coffee bars run by the division, constant training programs with the best consultants, employee 'success' retreats sponsored by the company. I'm telling you, people love working here. They have such a sense of dedication, of buy-in to the purposes of the organization. They love being part of this team."

Kyle finished a bite and had a drink of Coke. "Sounds almost too good to be true."

"It's the real thing." Logan paused a moment. "You know, Kyle, I've been meaning to ask you—what are you still doing on Level One?"

"What do you mean?"

"I mean exactly that. That place is a total waste of time."

Kyle had another bite before he answered. "Yeah, I know. It's the people. I really like hanging around some of them."

"But there are good people on every level."

"To be honest, none of the other levels has ever appealed to me. I can't go to Level Two—the rules would drive me nuts. Level Five's gotta be the same way, all the rules they must have being up there with top management. You said yourself that Level Three is kinda screwy."

"Come up here to Level Four. Trust me. You'll love it."

Kyle leaned back in his chair. "Well…maybe I should. Temporarily, anyway. Do you think you could arrange that?"

"I think so. Let me talk to the General Manager. I'm sure he could arrange for a temporary transfer. You could help me with my assignment and get someone to cover for you on Level One."

Two days later Kyle was on Level Four. He settled in at an empty desk next to Logan's. "I'm not here permanently, you know. All the stuff you said sounds great, but I'm not sure I'll go for the rah-rah about the Director and all the gung-ho stuff they do up here."

Logan laughed. "I don't know who is telling you that. Just give it a chance—that's all I'm asking."

## 10

THREE DAYS LATER LOGAN and Kyle sat in the Level Four auditorium with Angie, whom Logan had met at the Manual review. Although all Level Four employees were in attendance, the auditorium was less than half full. Still, the place rocked. A band hired by the General Manager was playing on the stage, leading the crowd in singing motivational songs. The words were flashed on a large screen with music video images streaming in the background. The crowd was clapping enthusiastically to the beat.

Angie leaned toward Logan and spoke loudly to be heard. "Isn't this great?"

"Yeah, pretty cool. I never thought I'd be at a concert at work."

They sang and clapped through four more songs before the General Manager took the stage. "Do you feel it?"

"Yessss!" the crowd replied.

"Do you feel it?!"

"YESSSS!"

"All right." He nodded to the band. "Let's give a big round of applause to the Universal Systems Profit Makers." The crowd cheered. "They do a great job every time we all get together.

"Okay. We have a lot to do today. Third-quarter profit figures are out, and I want to announce that our division's profit is up twenty-six percent over this period last year!"

A big cheer went up.

"You all have worked super hard, and you should be proud of the work you are doing for the Shareholder."

Another cheer.

"Next I want to announce that as a result of our earnings for the first three quarters of this year, the division is sponsoring a week-long cruise over the Christmas holiday!"

A huge cheer erupted and continued. The band started playing, and the whole crowd clapped and sang for five minutes. The noise finally died down as the GM motioned with his hand. "Now…" He waited for the crowd to fully settle. "Now, this isn't *just* a pleasure cruise."

Fake moans arose from the crowd.

"It'll be mostly pleasure." Applause again. "In addition, we have arranged for three outstanding motivational speakers to lead us during the week on the theme of 'Dreaming and Achieving Big Dreams for Yourself.' Plus—and we know you'll appreciate this opportunity—we have arranged a one-hour service project for the whole group at one of our stops."

Applause.

"Don't you really feel the spirit of the Shareholder in this place?"

"Yeeaaahhhh!" shouted the crowd.

"All right. We have a special treat for you this afternoon. Let me first ask this: how many visitors do we have from Levels One,

Two, and Three? Why don't you stand?" Fifty or so people stood to polite applause.

"We want to welcome you to the fourth level. We hope our monthly rally gives you a taste of what motivates us to excel and of the privilege we all feel in working for the Shareholder."

Logan noticed those around him nodding in agreement. Angie again leaned toward Logan and whispered, "Don't you love listening to him? I've never heard anyone who inspires me like he does."

The GM continued, "I'd like to start off with a testimonial from one of your co-workers, Jeff Millson. Jeff, come on up here."

A young man jogged down one of the aisles of the auditorium, climbed the stairs to the stage, and stood next to the GM.

"Jeff transferred up to us from Level One about…how long ago?"

"Six months."

"And what made you want to join the Level Four team?"

"I was just really dissatisfied on Level One. Everyone always doing whatever they wanted, no one contributing to the goals of the company. It felt real empty after a while. I mean, doing whatever you wanted was fun at first—don't get me wrong."

There was a smattering of laughter in the auditorium.

"But that finally gets old. Employment has to have more meaning than that. And I have found there's nothing more meaningful than working for the Shareholder and doing what he wants you to do."

The GM smiled broadly. "That's great, Jeff. Now tell us, have you been able to find a common bond with some of your work-mates in this division?"

"Absolutely. I feel like I've really connected with my work team, and my Manual review group—the camaraderie we share is incredible."

Angie touched Logan on the arm. "That's the way I feel about our Manual review group."

The GM wrapped up the interview. "Well, we are thrilled to have you up here with us. Give him a hand, folks."

The crowd applauded while Jeff headed off the stage.

"You see what a difference being on Level Four makes? We've all experienced it, we all know it, but unless we hear someone tell their story, we take for granted all that we have. Now, I want to be serious with you folks for a second."

The auditorium quieted.

"We need to have more visitors from Levels One, Two, and Three in these seats. Are people going to know what we know unless we invite them to see it for themselves?"

A couple of employees responded, "No."

"Let me hear you. Are they going to know?"

Most of the crowd shouted back, "No!"

"Are they going to experience what we experience unless we invite them to see it for themselves?"

"No!"

"All right, then. Here's my challenge. Today we have fifty or so visitors from down below. Next month I want us to increase that number to two hundred."

Angie and Logan glanced at each other, then Logan looked across Angie to Kyle, who mouthed, "Two hundred?"

"I want all of you to personally call or e-mail five people you know on Levels One through Three and invite them to come to our next rally. I want at least two hundred new faces in here. I know we can do it!"

There was applause and a few cheers from the crowd.

"Okay. I said that we have a treat for you this afternoon. I want to introduce a very special guest. You know him as Benny on the hit TV show *The Wild Side*. Before that, you knew him for his Grammy Award–winning country music. Please give a genuine Level Four welcome to Patrick Winstead!"

The auditorium exploded into cheers as the celebrity walked across the stage to the GM. After two or three minutes, the GM motioned for everyone to sit back down. "Now there's a Level Four welcome!"

He interviewed Winstead for about ten minutes. The entertainer told how the life principles of the Shareholder had rescued him from alcohol, a near divorce, and an endless string of bad investment decisions. "Now my personal life is back together, my marriage is better than ever, my kids are happy to have a real dad in the house, and the defined benefit pension plan that my accountant set up for me is going gangbusters."

He picked up his guitar, slid into a high-seated chair, and said, "I wrote this little tune for the Shareholder after I finally turned the corner."

He sang a soft melody, the end of which was greeted with

thunderous applause. The GM returned to center stage. "Patrick Winstead, everyone!" More applause as the singer left the stage. "Thank you, Patrick.

"All right. We want to conclude our program with our quarterly recommitment ceremony." Behind the GM, guys were moving chairs and large potted plants into place.

"Once a quarter we give all of you an opportunity to personally evaluate how you have been performing as Level Four employees. This is just between you and the Shareholder, what you think he expects of you. Are you fulfilling those expectations? Are you contributing to the goals of the company in the way you originally dedicated yourself to doing? Would the Shareholder be proud of your level of effort?"

Logan could feel Angie shifting in her seat next to him. The GM continued. "As they finish getting the stage ready, I want each of you in this auditorium to evaluate yourself. Are you being dedicated enough, or do you need to rededicate? Do you need to affirm once again to yourself, to your co-workers, and to the Shareholder your commitment to working for him?"

He turned and looked behind him. The new stage set was ready.

"All right. This is your time. If you feel the need to rededicate yourself, or even if you aren't sure but you might need to, come on down one of the aisles to the main stage here." Several people got up out of their seats and started moving to the aisles. "There you go. So many of us have done this. We all lag in our personal discipline and dedication at various times in our employment. We all understand. It's time to renew. It's time to work hard again. It's time to work smart again, to give it your best. Won't you come on down and rededicate yourself to the goals of the Shareholder?"

Logan felt a tap and saw Angie motioning for him to move his knees so she could get past. He looked around the auditorium. Several dozen employees were making their way down the aisles to the stage. Logan recognized one other—Curt, the Manual review leader.

Once on stage, they all took a seat. The GM motioned the employees to join him one by one. He thanked each for their contribution and for their personal courage in rededicating themselves. Each person spoke a few words of regret concerning their lack of commitment, then followed the GM in reciting a recommitment pledge.

After her turn, Angie shook the GM's hand and made her way back to her seat. Logan leaned over to her. "That was pretty brave."

He noticed tears in her eyes as she looked up at him. "It was time."

On the way out of the auditorium, everyone was handed a T-shirt with the slogan "One, Two, Three Up to Four: Get 200 Through the Door." Kyle slipped his on over his striped Burberry dress shirt. "Classy."

Back at their desks, Kyle walked over to Logan.

"So what did you think?" Logan asked.

"It was a little too rah-rah for me. And the recommitment ceremony just seemed too…"

"What?"

"Heavy-handed. That's a lot of pressure to put on people, if you ask me."

"I think it's good for employees to reaffirm their commitment to a goal. That's all they were doing."

"But they mentioned that some of those people had already rededicated themselves three quarters in a row. Maybe dedication isn't their problem." Kyle glanced at some other employees returning to their desks. "Something else. What about everyone up there talking about how they know the Shareholder personally? Let me ask you—has anyone ever actually met the Shareholder?"

Logan shrugged. "That's a good question. I don't know."

## 11

THE NEXT WEEK LOGAN and Kyle attended an all-day training seminar that featured a group of consultants who came in about once a year. The seminar was entitled "Participating in the Plans of the Shareholder." There were morning and afternoon group-wide training sessions with slick PowerPoint presentations laced with film clips, plus four breakout sessions with workshops.

Along with Ben, Logan chose workshop schedule A:

✓ Success Secrets of the Shareholder

✓ Your Best Career Now

✓ How to E-mail the Director and Get What You Want

✓ Expanding the Vision of What You Can Have

Kyle opted for workshop schedule B:

✓ Leadership Secrets of the Director

✓ Lessons from the Director in Achieving Your Personal Goals

✓ Developing a Healthy Professional Self-Image

✓ Receiving All That the Shareholder Intends for You

During the midday break they perused the book table in the back of the main room. Ben bought four books, the CD set of the training session, and a DVD series called *Bringing Out the Champion in You: Professional Disciplines for Those Climbing the Ladder.* Logan ordered the CD set. Kyle passed on everything.

"Why don't you get something?" Logan asked Kyle as they waited for Ben to finish his purchase.

"What for?"

"This is good stuff. It can't hurt, you know."

"Yes it can. It can hurt my pocketbook." Kyle lowered his voice. "Have you seen the bookshelf Ben already has full of this stuff? I bet he has a two thousand dollar collection sitting right there at his desk."

Following the afternoon session, the three of them went to the coffee bar to compare notes. Logan offered his opinion first. "I thought the first presentation was great. *The Matrix* clips made me think—reality is often not what it seems. I liked the testimonials about trusting the Director to help you achieve your goals, since he wants us to succeed professionally."

Kyle took a bite into a large orange-flavored scone. "What about your workshops, Ben? Any of them worth anything?"

"All of them. I couldn't stop jotting down action points during the talk on success secrets. And the one on thinking bigger about what you could have—that really hit the mark. I need to think bigger." He reached over and grabbed a napkin from Kyle's stack. "What about your sessions?"

"They were interesting. The *Braveheart* clips kept me awake." Kyle glanced over at Logan, who rolled his eyes.

Ben spoke again. "I wish they'd had more specific steps to take for professional development. I guess…well, do you two mind if I get honest with you for a second?"

"No," they both replied.

"I feel like my career needs a jump-start right now. I've been in the same job for four years with no promotion. I came to Level Four expecting frequent advancement, but that hasn't happened. Maybe the DVD set I got will have some good stuff on that."

Ben put down his latte. "I guess you could say I'm a little burned out on all the ways we're supposed to improve ourselves here. None of it seems to be working for me. I've been doing everything I know to do, but I'm not really progressing. I'm certainly not living up to what these speakers say."

Kyle placed both hands around his coffee cup. "Do you think anyone else is, either?"

"Everyone acts like they are."

They finished their drinks and walked back to their work area. Kyle sat in one of Logan's chairs.

"I thought it was your job to find out what the main problem is on every level."

"It is."

"And have you found it here?"

"Not really. I guess for a while I didn't think there was a problem."

"For a while? You're still acting like the head cheerleader for this place."

"I'm still assessing."

"It sounds to me like there's plenty to assess."

Logan and Kyle spent the next week interviewing a wide variety of Level Four personnel—managers, professionals, technicians, and administrative support. The sessions grew tedious after a couple of days, but the details often caught their attention. They noticed that Level Four employees were big on slogans. Screen savers, plaques, bumper stickers on the sides of computers—they always carried a motivational message. Logan and Kyle were surprised to find that some employees had a screen saver with a picture of the Director and the phrase "Work to the Fullest" at the top. *Why would the Director have a screen saver made of himself?* Logan wondered.

Level Four people also seemed to be quite fond of stuff. They always had a lot around them: CDs to listen to while they worked, headphones, stacks of motivational DVDs, company trinkets on their desks, and company posters if they had walls. Logan thought more than once, *Where do they get all of this?*

Everyone was committed. At least they kept telling Logan and Kyle about their level of commitment and their sacrifices for the Shareholder. Despite all the talk about commitment, however, from what Logan could tell, employees on Level Four worked pretty much as did employees on Levels Two and Three. They participated in different activities (the pep rallies, the Manual reviews, and such), but when Logan observed their day-to-day work, it was hard to distinguish them from Level Two or Three.

Level Four employees highly valued what they received as a result of working on Level Four: good pay, recognition, and, of course, a guaranteed job forever. That was quite a perk.

Most of all, virtually everyone said they were happy. They were happy with their jobs, the Director, the Shareholder, one another. They were happy to be working for the best division of the best company.

"People here claim to be happy," Logan commented to Kyle.

"Yeah. I picked up on that."

Friday morning Kyle left his work area to meet Ben at a coffee bar. Logan took the opportunity for a vending machine break. He passed by a conference room and noticed Angie sitting at the table, looking distraught. He popped his head inside the door.

"Everything okay?"

Angie looked up. Her mascara was smeared.

Logan took a seat at the table. "What's wrong?"

"I just got a call…"

He leaned over and got her a tissue from a small table against the wall. She wiped her eyes.

"…from a client. They were going to sign a big contract with us, but now they've given the business to someone else." She dabbed her eyes again. "I know this is silly. It's just that I was really counting on that deal."

Logan stayed silent for a moment. "I'm sorry."

Angie picked up her cell phone off the table and placed it in her purse. "Thanks. I didn't mean to unload this on you."

"No, that's okay. I understand."

"I just don't get why they backed out. It was a done deal as far as I knew. Why would the Director let that happen? I e-mailed him about it and asked him to talk to their general manager directly and seal the deal. I figured he had, but maybe he didn't. I trusted him. I trusted him to make sure this would happen. Now all the work I put into it is ruined. Everything is ruined."

Tears started down her cheeks again. Logan offered her another tissue. "I wish I had the answers for you," he said between her sobs. "I don't know that much about how the Director works, I suppose."

She looked up at him. "Yeah, I know what you mean. I thought I did. But"—she wiped off some more mascara—"I'm not sure he's what I want him to be. He doesn't seem to do what I want. Why doesn't he do what I want?"

In the coffee bar, Ben took a seat opposite Kyle. "How have the interviews been going this week for you and Logan?"

"Not bad. They get a little routine after a while. Most everyone says the same thing. It's almost…" Kyle paused.

"What?"

"It's almost like they're saying what they are supposed to say."

"Are you implying they're being told what to say?"

"No, not at all. It's just… It's like this. You go to something that's supposed to be great. Senior prom is a good example. Everybody goes, and afterward everyone says how great it was. You may have had a pretty mediocre time. I certainly did. But you don't tell anyone that. Someone asks you about it, and you say, 'It was great.'"

"You think that's what you've been hearing?"

"Yeah. Partly. I don't think things are as great on this level as everyone says they are."

Ben raised an eyebrow. "What makes you say that?"

"For one, they're always talking about how they love working for the Shareholder and the Director and how they love putting forth extra effort for their sakes. But I don't see that."

"You don't think anyone here is excited about his job?"

"A few are. The rest—it's just a job. They do it because they're supposed to, not because they love doing it for anyone's sake. Another thing. I think people get tired of all the Level Four mantras."

"Mantras? What mantras?"

"'We are the most committed in the company.' 'We do everything the Shareholder wants us to do.' 'We're the only ones doing everything he wants us to do.' 'We experience work to the fullest.' 'The Director is our best friend.' Let me ask you a question. Do you consider the Director to be your best friend?"

"Well, you're right. That's kind of what we're expected to say."

"But is it true?"

"Not for me, no."

Kyle leaned back. "I suppose I just see a lot of superficiality. People saying and doing things because that's the culture, not because their heart is in it. I'm not talking about you personally."

"That's fine."

"Everyone is supposedly so happy on this level. But I just see a lot of people staying really busy and convincing themselves that they are happy because Level Four employees are supposed to be. In the meantime, they go to seminars and watch motivational DVDs to make themselves more fulfilled. Or they play computer games to distract themselves. And all the while they are allegedly doing everything the Shareholder wants them to. There's just too much of a disconnect."

Ben was silent for what seemed like forever. Finally he spoke. "You know, Kyle, you're pretty astute for someone from Level One."

Kyle laughed. "Well, that's just what I've observed. I may be wrong. I tend to jump to conclusions too fast sometimes."

"No, I think you're pretty right-on."

"I don't mean this as a slam on you in any way. Frankly, you're the most real person I've met up here."

Ben smiled briefly. "Thanks." He leaned forward and spoke more quietly. "To tell you the truth, I feel kind of disillusioned about the whole thing. I think a lot of us do. But no one will admit it. We do all the things we've been told are important to do—our jobs, the Manual reviews, our personal Manual reading, listening to motivational stuff. There's a whole lot of activity going on, but where are the results? Working here never lives up to all the hype. No one experiences 'work to the fullest,' not as I would define it, anyway."

"So why doesn't anyone do things differently?"

"What else is there to do? How we do things here is supposed to be the absolute best way to do them. That's what the Manual says, as far as I can tell."

"Maybe people aren't reading the Manual right."

Ben shook his head. "If this isn't what the Shareholder wants us to be doing, what is?"

Kyle leaned closer and spoke more quietly himself. "I've been meaning to ask you this question for a while. Has anyone ever actually seen the Shareholder?"

Ben glanced to the left and right. "Not that I know of."

"How do you know he really exists?"

Ben looked down at the table, then back up at Kyle. "Sometimes I wonder about that myself. But how could we have a company like Universal Systems without an owner?"

At lunch Logan and Kyle discussed their morning encounters. Logan was surprised at the things Ben had told Kyle. "I guess I never expected him to feel that way. Or tell anyone if he did."

Kyle nodded. "I think he's come to realize that, for him, this level isn't all it's cracked up to be, although he's still trying hard to make it that way. Logan, we've been doing interviews all week. What do you think of Level Four at this point?"

"Let's just say my eyes are opening a bit."

That afternoon Logan ran into Curt, his Manual review leader, at a copy machine. Curt was finishing the first of two brownies he had brought with him.

"I thought you were on a diet."

"I need some comfort food."

"For what?"

"Didn't you hear about the market today?"

"No, what happened?"

"The Dow is down over two percent. That's on top of the four percent loss last week. In the last month it has given back its entire gain for the year. I have to earn nine percent on my investments to reach my financial targets. Everything depends on that, like my kids' college tuition. Now I'll have to earn over seventeen percent next year just to average out. What's the chance of that happening?" Curt downed his second brownie in one bite.

"But I heard that the Shareholder promises to provide whatever you need."

"Yeah, well, maybe. But who knows what that covers—a public university probably. Or helping you fill out the forms for student loans."

"A lot of students go those routes. Most, actually."

"Not my kids. Not if I can help it, they won't. I don't want them going to State. How are they going to climb to the top that way?"

Having downed all his calories, Curt grabbed his copies and departed. Logan walked back toward his desk. He stopped at Kyle's and sat in a chair.

"Finished for the day?" Kyle asked.

"Maybe finished for this level."

"You've given up?"

"No. I think I know what's wrong with Level Four."

# 12

CROSSING LEVEL FIVE, LOGAN noticed that the conference table was full again. *They seem to gather first thing in the morning and at the end of the day,* he thought. *I wonder what they do the rest of the time.*

"I think I have Level Four figured out," Logan stated after sitting down across from the Director.

"That's impressive. Level Four is a tough nut to crack."

"Well, partially figured out. By the way, that screen saver of you is pretty cool."

The Director laughed. "There's a screen saver of me somewhere?"

"On Level Four."

The Director shook his head. "Well, I've been trying to get them to pay more attention to me down there. Maybe that's the answer." The Director placed his forearms on his desk. "So what have you concluded about Level Four?"

"At first I thought that Level Four was the perfect place. Almost perfect, anyway. They seemed to be doing everything you wanted them to do. And everyone seemed happy with their work."

"And then?"

"Then I started getting to know the place better, and the people, and somehow—I'm not exactly sure how—Level Four is just like Levels One, Two, and Three, isn't it? I don't mean exactly like them, because they do know what's going on with you and the Shareholder, and they do seem intent on working for the Shareholder, but…"

"But?"

"Why does it seem to me they're just doing their own thing, like the other levels? It's as if they're partly in line with the company's goals and partly not. I'm not quite sure how to explain it."

"It is confusing, isn't it? But your gut instinct is right. People on Level Four are basically operating on their own, not in accord with the Shareholder."

"But how can that be? They're trying hard to do what the Shareholder wants them to do, aren't they?"

The Director shifted back in his chair. "Well, they are trying hard, that's for certain. The issue is, whose goals are they ultimately trying to achieve—the Shareholder's or their own?"

"Maybe they don't know the difference."

"Ah. Very insightful. The truth is, those on Level Four do think the Shareholder is important, and they really do want to accomplish his goals. But they want to do so within the context of accomplishing their own goals. It's like the Shareholder is another piece of pie that they are trying to wedge into an already full pie—the pie of their own aims. An extra piece of pie just makes the whole thing too crowded. It gets burdensome. It takes the joy out of it all, trying to work for both yourself and the Shareholder. You really have to choose one or the other."

"I can't believe I'm saying this, but it seems like some on Level One are happier than a number of the people I met on Level Four."

"In a sense they are. They don't have that conflict. They're not trying to work for themselves and for someone else. They're only here for themselves. It's easier—for a while at least."

Logan thought for a moment. "I don't think you're saying those on Level Four are insincere."

The Director shook his head. "Not at all. Quite genuine, in fact. They are simply divided. They want to work for the Shareholder, but by and large, work still revolves around them—what they want to do, what their goals are, whether they are getting what they want." Logan thought of Angie's tears over losing a client and Curt's financial worries. The Director continued, "As long as they are the center, they're fooling themselves. The Shareholder's agenda is not really their own."

"So I'm curious. Is Level Four making a profit for us?"

The Director reached into a drawer and handed Logan a folder. Logan looked at the profit and loss statements of Level Four. "So they do make a small profit. But it isn't enough to off-set all the losses from Levels One, Two, and Three. Does the company as a whole post a loss every year?"

"No, we have a profit every year."

"We do? Who produces the profit?"

The Director pointed to the group sitting around the conference table in the distance. "They do."

## 13

"ONE CONFERENCE TABLE is producing Universal Systems' profit?"

"Yes."

"How can that be? What are they doing that all the people on Level Four aren't doing?"

"How about if I let you figure that out? You're the organizational development man."

"Is this a final test?"

"No. You finished your original assignment. Consider this one optional. If you'd like to find out, you're welcome to look into it."

"Of course I'd like to. It sounds like the whole company rests on this issue."

The Director smiled. "You could say that, couldn't you?" He rose, and Logan followed. "Tomorrow I'll arrange for you to spend time with some of the Level Five group. Be here when the conference table meeting adjourns."

The next morning at 8:30, Logan met Grady Wilson, a Level Five employee. Logan accompanied him down to his work on Level Three. They wound through the expanse until they came to the work station of Lana Mahoney, a debugging specialist. She was not at her desk. Grady pulled up a couple of chairs for himself and Logan and opened a filing cabinet.

"This is not going to be too exciting, you know. Watching someone file."

"Is that what you do—administrative assistant work?"

"I was a facilities engineering manager on Level Four."

"And now you're filing?"

"I'm good at organizing. Lana needs help with her files."

"Isn't it a little boring?"

"By itself, maybe. But nothing is really boring when I do it for the Director."

"What do you mean?"

"When I do this for the Director, and for Lana, I throw myself into it and have joy in the task. In its own way it's more fulfilling than what I did on Level Four, because I am helping produce the ultimate product."

After a while Logan returned to Level Five. The conference table was empty. Logan walked to the Director's desk.

"How was your time with Grady?"

"A little surprising." He sat in one of the chairs. "Who's next on my list?"

They mapped out an agenda for the rest of the day. Logan joined several more Level Five employees. The first was working as a trainer on Level Two, the second as a procurement manager on Level Three, and the third as a Web designer on Level Four. They all had pretty much the same story—they worked in each of their positions temporarily as a need existed, then they moved on to another assignment. They all returned to the Level Five conference table for an end-of-the-day meeting.

The most unusual job Logan observed was that of Sara Creighton. A Dr Pepper in hand, Logan joined her in the cafeteria on Level One.

"What do you do down here?"

"I sit in the cafeteria."

"All day?"

"Pretty much. I take a walk when I need a break."

"So what do…"

"I do in the cafeteria?"

"Yeah."

"I wait for employees to come talk to me."

"That's it? You sit here until someone comes to talk to you?"

"Yes."

"Who comes to talk to you?"

"Anyone who wants to. They all know I am here."

Logan found this job description mystifying. "What do people come talk to you about?"

"Whatever they want to. Their lives. Their stress. Working on Level One is hard, you know."

"But they don't do anything down here. They just do whatever they want. They goof off all day."

"Yes. And it wears them out. It's an unfulfilling way to work, with yourself at the center, never contributing toward something bigger than yourself."

"What do you tell them?"

"I listen mostly. I remind them of their worth, that they are important to top management. I counsel them sometimes concerning their situation."

"Does it ever help?"

"Sometimes it helps an immediate crisis. Of course, I tell them there is a long-term solution to their issue but they can't find it on this level."

"You invite them to come up to Level Five?"

"Yes."

"Do any of them take you up on it?"

"Not too many. Every once in a while, though. In fact, a woman recently—" She looked over Logan's head to a young man who had walked up.

"Are you Sara?"

"Yes."

"I'm sorry to interrupt. I can come back."

Logan stood. "No, I'll let you two talk. Sara, good to meet you."

"You too."

He returned to Level Five. The conference table was still empty. The Director saw Logan and motioned for him to join him.

"So, end of your first day on Level Five. How did it go?"

"Fine, I guess. I mean, I really enjoyed being with everyone. This level seems pretty simple."

"It is. In what way are you thinking?"

"It's all about serving those who need help."

The Director smiled. "Well, that's what you're seeing on the surface, yes. But that's not the deepest dynamic of the level. You'll find there's more here than meets the eye." He pointed toward a room in the distance that Logan had not yet visited. "You might be interested in talking to someone in there. He'll be an exception to your conclusion. Half the time, at least. But he's not an exception to what Level Five is about."

Logan walked over to the room, which he discovered was a library filled with volumes from floor to ceiling and furnished with upholstered armchairs and sofas. A young man sat reading a book in one of the chairs.

He looked up at Logan. "Hello."

"Hello. I am supposed to talk to someone in here."

"I'm the only one here, so that must be me." He stood and stuck out his hand. "Ryan Davis."

"Logan Bell."

The young man sat back down in his chair; Logan took the edge of a sofa.

"So what brings you over here to meet me?"

"I'm spending time with Level Five employees, seeing what they do."

"Oh, you're the OD guy the Director hired."

"Right."

"Cool. Well, I've been doing pretty much what you see." He held up a book. "Reading. I love to read."

"What are you reading?"

"*The Brothers Karamazov.* Dostoevsky."

"Have you been here all day?"

"In the mornings I do graphic design on Level Two. After lunch I come in here."

"Does the Director know about this?"

Ryan laughed. "Of course. This is the assignment he gave me. Or you could say this is what he invited me to do."

"He did? He tells you to come in here and read?"

"Yes."

"Why?"

"I asked him, but he didn't really give me a straight answer. He just told me to trust him on this one."

"Are you in here by yourself all afternoon?"

"No, the Shareholder usually drops by and spends some time."

"Really?" Logan tried to hide his surprise. "What does he do?"

"Talk with me."

"He does? About what?"

"Whatever we want. We just chat."

"Don't take this the wrong way, but why does the Shareholder do that with you personally?"

"I don't know. He likes to, I guess. I like it too, actually. He's become a kind of personal mentor to me." Ryan glanced down at his watch. "Oh, it's almost five. We'd better head back in."

"For what?"

"Our end-of-the-day meeting. I imagine you're welcome to join us."

They walked to the conference table. Seats were filling up.

Logan was introduced to a number of persons he had not previously met. One, John, had just arrived at work.

"You just got here?" Logan inquired.

"I work the night shift."

"What do you do?"

"Right now I help the janitorial crew clean up the place."

"What do they have you clean?"

He grinned. "Bathrooms mostly. New man on the crew."

Everyone was seated when the last person approached the table. Logan instantly recognized her.

"Beth! What are you doing here? Do you work on Level Five?"

"Hi, Logan." She smiled at him. "I do now." As she sat at the table, Logan noticed that she was showing much less cleavage than before.

"Since when?"

"A couple of weeks ago."

"How did you make it up here?"

She gave a slight shrug. "Anyone can work up here."

The meeting began. For a business meeting, it was odd. They didn't talk about any regular business stuff, Logan thought. Instead, they briefly discussed what each of them had done that day, highlighting their interactions with employees on the various levels. They then talked about the needs of specific individuals throughout the organization and also how they could support each other for the next day, both personally and professionally.

As everyone walked away from the table, Beth and Logan remained seated.

"Beth," Logan started, "I just wanted to…"

"No, first I want to apologize to you."

"Apologize? For what?"

"For the way I acted toward you on Level One."

"What? You mean…"

"Yeah. For coming on to you."

"Well, it was a little fast, but I wasn't exactly uninterested, you know."

"I know. Still, it was wrong of me. Will you accept my apology?"

Logan wasn't used to responding to that kind of request, but he gave what seemed like the reasonable response. "Sure. No problem. I mean, cool."

He placed his arms on the table and intertwined his fingers. "I'm really curious. What are you doing up here on Level Five? This would be the last place I'd expect you to be—no offense."

"No, not at all. Before, it would have been. Sara Creighton offered me the opportunity. Do you know her?"

"I just met her this morning on Level One. You must have talked with her."

"Several times. I felt like things were just getting real messed up—at work, in my personal life, in everything. She was a good listening ear."

"What did she tell you?"

"She told me there was a level where I could be free from all that."

"It looked to me like you were having quite a bit of fun down there."

"I guess. Living like that is always fun for a while. And then reality sets in. It doesn't make you happy. It doesn't produce anything worthwhile. It doesn't help anyone. It doesn't make you feel good about yourself. Other than that, it's great."

"But being up here… Do you really want the jobs they force you to do?"

Beth laughed out loud.

"What?" Logan asked. "What's so funny?"

"What you said. No one forces us to do anything up here. We are free to do whatever we want."

"But you all do whatever the Shareholder wants you to do."

"Yes, but that's our choice. That is ultimate freedom, to be able to fulfill our purpose. Not many do."

"But could you choose not to?"

"Of course. I told you, we are free up here. We use our freedom to be an expression of the Shareholder, you might say. People look at us and are able to say, 'That's how the Shareholder operates.' That's what we were all hired to do, you know."

"You mean here on Level Five?"

"No, I mean everyone in the company. It's just that very few choose to do that. Instead, they work for themselves, for their own aims."

"I know. But you're saying you don't work that way anymore?"

"No, I don't. I'm working for the sake of the Shareholder. My goal is to accomplish his purpose, not mine."

Logan thought for a moment. "I don't know if I could ever do that."

"Then you'll never experience work to the fullest."

"The fullest what?"

"Meaning. Purpose. Significance. Fulfillment."

Logan shook his head. "I don't know. This is just...too radical. Who wants to give up their freedom like you have?"

Beth smiled and placed her hands on the table. "Logan, you're completely missing it. I haven't given up any freedom at all. I am free as I've never been before. Working with yourself at the center—grabbing for yourself, acquiring for yourself, scheming and manipulating for yourself, protecting yourself, worrying for yourself, worrying about what others think of you—how exactly is that freedom?"

# 14

THE NEXT MORNING LOGAN gave Kyle a call. "You'll never believe who's working on Level Five now."

"Who?"

"Beth."

"Beth from down here?"

"The one and only."

"I wondered where she had transferred to. How many of her come-ons have you had to fight off?"

"None. I don't think she does that anymore. She's totally changed."

"For the better?"

"I'm not sure yet. To tell you the truth, I haven't figured out anything on this level yet. It doesn't make any sense to me."

"So you're not calling to recommend I transfer up there?"

Logan laughed. "Not until I decipher this level. When I'm ready to recommend anything, you'll be the first to know."

"Hey, have you told your dad you're up on Level Five now?"

"Yeah. He's not too impressed."

"Why not?"

"I think he's kind of disappointed that I'm still hopping levels, as he calls it. He knows the GM on Level Three. Thinks I should go to work for her."

"Are you considering it?"

"Who knows? Once I finish this assignment, I'm not sure what the Director has planned for me."

That afternoon just before 5:00, Logan ran into John, the night-shift janitor, in the fifth floor kitchen. Logan waited as he put his sack dinner in the refrigerator.

"Do you mind if I ask you a question?"

"No, go ahead."

"What did you do before you started cleaning bathrooms?"

"My primary job at Universal Systems has been as a risk-assessment manager."

Logan opened the door as they headed back toward the conference table. "That's quite a switch."

John chuckled. "Not really. I have to assess risk every time I stick my hand inside a toilet bowl."

They both laughed.

"Can I ask you an even more personal question?"

"Sure."

"Are you getting paid the same as you used to?"

"No. I'm getting paid what the janitorial staff gets paid."

Logan stared at him. "So…so you're making a fraction of what you used to?"

"Yes."

"Why? Why would you accept such a huge pay cut?"

"Because that's what the Director does. That's what he did for us—sacrificed himself. And now he enables us to do the same thing. That's what we're here for. Our lives as employees are completely his, to reflect him."

"But it doesn't make any sense."

"It makes perfect sense. How could I serve with the janitorial staff and be one of them while making five or six times what they earn? To serve them, I had to become like them."

"But it's not fair."

John smiled. "No, it isn't. It isn't fair that I do some small tasks for the Shareholder, and in return I get everything. I'd say I have a pretty good deal."

Logan observed Level Five for another week. He sat in on all conference table meetings. The group seemed to rely on each other heavily. "We could never do this on our own" was a statement he heard several times.

After a while Logan saw the need for the mutual support. In the midst of the peacefulness of Level Five, he noticed that difficulties in their work were frequent, from the "counseling" situations Sara encountered on Level One to the repeated occasions of Level Fivers being misunderstood on Level Four. "They think we're weird, that we have the attitude that we don't have to do all the things they do, like Manual reviews," explained one person. "For their sake, we try to do as much of it as we can."

Individuals frequently spent time with the Director, either one-on-one or in small groups. Often the Director would join the conference table gathering; sometimes he would not. "He seems to have an uncanny sense of when we need his input and when we need to hash out things ourselves or just encourage one another as peers," Sara told Logan.

Another frequent attendee at the conference table gathering, someone whom Logan had not met before, was the company's Chief Counsel. On Level Five, he was affectionately known as the Advisor. "He's related to the Shareholder somehow," someone had told Logan on Level Four. Apparently the Advisor had been instrumental in starting the company. He had transitioned into a troubleshooting role on all levels but directed a considerable portion of his attention to Level Five.

Gradually Logan realized that what seemed to set Level Five people apart was not commitment or activity (many Level Four employees were committed and energetic in their efforts) but outlook. As they put it, they had adopted the outlook of the Director. "We see the company, and our part in it, as he and the Shareholder see it. He isn't a part of our plan; we are part of his."

On the elevator one morning, Logan ran into Grady heading down to do more filing.

"Don't you ever get tired of doing things for the Shareholder?" Logan asked.

"If that's primarily what we were doing—things *for* the Shareholder—it would wear anyone out, I suppose. But that's not really what we're doing. We allow him to operate the company through us. He empowers us every step along the way."

Logan nodded. "If there's one thing I learned in school, it's the importance of empowering employees to act independently."

Grady smiled to himself and shook his head.

"What?"

"Empowerment here is the opposite. The Shareholder and the Director empower us not to independence but to dependence."

"On who?"

"The two of them."

"I'm not following you."

"I'm not sure I can explain it to you. It simply has to be experienced. The Shareholder and the Director operate the company as they wish, and somehow they enable us to operate that way too. I didn't experience this on any other level. None of us did."

"So what's happening on the other four levels?"

"I guess you could say they're operating on their own efforts. But we aren't. Our ability comes from the two of them."

Logan asked several others about this, but he never got an answer that was any clearer. "The Shareholder and the Director are the fuel of this level" was the consistent refrain.

After a week and a half on Level Five, Logan was no closer to figuring out how such a small group could generate the bulk of the company's profit. He hadn't given up, though. From his interactions and observations on Level Five, Logan had gradually accumulated a list of questions. He returned to the Director's desk.

"Go ahead," the Director invited him. "Ask away."

Logan glanced at his PDA. "Okay, here goes. Is it true that anyone can come work on Level Five?"

"Yes, that is true."

"What do you have to commit to?"

"You don't have to commit to anything. But you must have the Shareholder's outlook on the company."

"And yours."

"And mine."

Logan shifted in his seat and glanced at his PDA again. "People up here talk like they know the Shareholder well."

"They do."

"But fourth level employees talk that way too."

"Yes." The Director paused. "They know him too. Just not well."

"Why? Because he's up here on Level Five?"

"Level Five people do have direct access to him. But so do those on Level Four, if they choose to. That's not the main difference."

"What is?"

"The difference is that the Level Five group is completely on the same page as the Shareholder—his page, so to speak. His aims have become theirs. They know him well because they are pulling in the same direction, not in competing directions. Haven't you ever experienced that?"

Logan thought about that for a moment. "I suppose I have. In high school, on the newspaper staff. We really got to know each other well, producing that paper. Is that what you're talking about?"

The Director leaned back and intertwined his fingers behind his head. "In a sense. What I'm referring to, though, is a common mindset, not a common product. Level Five has the Shareholder's frame of reference. That's why they know him well."

"But it seems like those on Level Four are also trying hard to do what he wants, with all their Manual reviews and so forth."

"Those things are fine, but they won't help them know the Shareholder very well."

"Why not?"

"Because their mindset is mostly at cross-purposes with his. As long as they are working for the sake of themselves, doing what they want to do, only working for the Shareholder on their own terms—in other words, as long as they are the center—they can't really know him well. Knowing someone well requires being completely on the same team."

That was the second time the Director had made that point. It had surprised Logan to hear it the first time, and it surprised him now. He entered something in his PDA and paused for a couple of seconds. "Okay, a question for you personally. What would you say your purpose is in the company?"

"My purpose is to make Universal Systems everything the Shareholder wants it to be. I want it to reflect well on him. Ultimately, my goal is to accomplish his profit goal. That's what I enjoy doing."

"You seem to really like working for him."

The Director smiled. "You might say that. Everything I do here is for his sake. One day this whole company will be running on all cylinders. Every level will be like Level Five. I can't imagine anything making him happier."

Logan looked down and scrolled through his PDA once more. "That's about it, I suppose."

"Very good questions." The Director started to rise.

"Oh, I did have one more. This isn't the most important issue, I guess, and I hate to pry into someone's personal business…"

"Ask anything. That's what you're here for."

"I'm curious as to why a guy here on Level Five, Ryan, spends his afternoons reading in the library."

The Director chuckled. "That is a bit unusual, isn't it? That was the Shareholder's decision. He knows Ryan loves to do that, so he gave him that option. It makes him happy."

"It makes Ryan happy?"

"It makes the Shareholder happy."

They both rose and took a few steps away from the desk. The Director spoke. "Do you feel any closer to figuring things out yet?"

"No, not really. I feel like I'm learning a lot of things about Level Five, but the heart of it, what's really happening up here—it's just hard to get my brain around it."

"Well, it's not a race. You can take your time."

They took a few more steps, and Logan glanced across the vast floor. He saw something he had never noticed before. "What is that way over there?"

"What is what?"

"It looks like an office. I didn't think there were any offices on Level Five."

"There is one. That's the Shareholder's office."

"That's the Shareholder's office? He stays here?"

"That surprises you?"

"I just figured…I don't know…that he was off site or something."

"No, not at all. Would you like to meet him?"

"I could? I mean, could I?"

"Of course. He'd be happy to chat. Go on over."

"Right now? Shouldn't I make an appointment?"

"You never make one with me, do you?"

"I know, but…"

"But he's more important?" The Director laughed.

"I didn't mean…"

"That's all right. I think now is a great time. He'll enjoy meeting you."

"Do you want to come and introduce us?"

"You can introduce yourself. He's heard of you."

"He has?" Logan glanced toward the lone office again. "All right."

Logan started the long walk across Level Five, unsure what to expect from the enigmatic Shareholder.

## 15

THE DOOR TO THE SHAREHOLDER'S OFFICE was open. Logan paused in the doorway when he saw that the Shareholder was on the phone. The Shareholder spotted him and motioned for him to take a seat while he finished his conversation.

The Shareholder's office was spacious with a classic feel to it. Logan looked around at the large, uncluttered granite-topped desk, the matching desk-hutch behind it, two large bookcases, and two brown easy chairs for guests. The walls were adorned with original landscapes.

The Shareholder himself looked trim, perhaps athletic in years past. He wore a gray suit, a yellow paisley tie, and copper-colored wire glasses.

Logan couldn't help listening to the Shareholder's side of the conversation. "He inherits the whole thing, of course... Yes... Right. I want all of them to inherit it as well... No, not divided up. All of them get to receive the whole thing."

There was a long pause as the Shareholder listened, then responded. "Bill, I know the provisions are unusual, but I'm confident you can make it happen. Use that wonderful creativity of yours. Chew on it, and call me back if you need anything more on my end... Okay... Thanks."

He hung up and turned to Logan. "Excuse me for the delay. My attorney and I keep going back and forth about my will." He stood and extended his hand. "They call me the Shareholder."

"I'm Logan Bell. I've been working—"

"For the Director. I know. You're the organizational analyst."

"Yes sir."

"Have you diagnosed the first four levels yet?"

Logan was surprised that the Shareholder knew so much about his work. "Yes, I have. Now I'm working on the fifth level."

"You won't find too many problems."

"I know. Just trying to figure out why it produces all, or most, of our profit."

"Ah. A very good question indeed. Have you figured it out yet?"

"No, not yet."

"I'm not surprised. It's counterintuitive, you might say. Can I offer you something to drink?"

"I'd love a—water would be great."

The Shareholder walked over to a small refrigerator in a nook of the office and grabbed a bottle. "It's a delight to have you as part of the team, Logan. How long have you been with us now?" He walked back across the room and handed the water to Logan.

"About three months."

The Shareholder sat back in his chair. "You've had a chance to sample every division here. What do you think of our fair company?"

Logan took a deep breath. "Well, it's different, that's for sure. I suppose you want me to be honest."

"Of course. No point in being anything else."

"Levels One through Four—they have some really nice folks…"

"Yes, they do."

"But they're all just doing their own thing, not yours."

"At this time, yes."

"Why do you keep them on the payroll?"

The Shareholder smiled. "Those levels are training grounds. When it comes to being a productive part of our team, most people have to go through how it doesn't work before they're ready for how it does work. Levels One through Four are how it doesn't work."

"But almost everyone is on those levels."

"For now. Have you noticed all the empty desks on Level Five, though?"

"It's hard to miss them."

"Eventually every desk on this level will be filled. There won't be an empty space on the whole floor."

"I thought that was happening on Level Four."

The Shareholder shook his head. "Hardly. Can you imagine the long-term mess that would be—everyone still devoted to themselves on Level Four?"

"When will Level Five be filled?"

"When people are committed to our goals, not their own."

"What will they all be doing up here one day?"

"They will do what everyone on Level Five does—let me produce this company's main product through them."

Logan took a sip of his water. "To be honest, I don't see how the few employees on Level Five produce any profit at all. I mean, they don't even stay up here during the day. They go down to the other levels and help them out. I don't see that this level even has a visible product."

The Shareholder grinned. "True enough. Level Five has no visible product. But it does have an invisible one."

Logan stared at him. "What? What does that mean?"

"The true product of this company is self-giving, other-focused love. My son and I started offering it, just the two of us. Now there are others on Level Five who are producing it as well. In a sense, they are extensions of the two of us. One day the floor will be overflowing with people producing it."

Logan was incredulous. "Love? That's our product?"

"Yes. The kind we provide is unique. People from all over the world get it from us."

"But…but…how do you make a profit from that?"

The Shareholder leaned forward and rested his forearms on his desk. "The real question, Logan, is this: how do you profit without it? You see, in this company if you hold on to what you want for yourself, it produces a loss. But if you give yourself up for the sake of the company—for myself and my son—then it produces huge profits. And you personally gain everything."

Logan spent a moment processing what he had just heard. He looked down at his PDA. "You mentioned your son a couple of times."

"Yes. My greatest joy is being able to give this company to him. I've built the whole thing for his sake. I want it to perfectly reflect who he is. He is the best example of self-giving, other-focused love that I know."

"Is he part of it now? I don't recall being introduced to him."

"You've spoken with him many times."

"I have? Who is he?"

"The Director. The Director is my son."

Logan couldn't believe he had missed that before. Now it seemed so obvious. "So when you were talking to your attorney about someone—" He stopped. "I'm sorry, I shouldn't have been eavesdropping."

"No, that's quite all right. I invited you in. My will is no secret around here."

Logan breathed more easily. "Okay. So when you referred to someone inheriting the whole thing, you were talking about the Director?"

"Of course. Despite its size, Universal Systems is a family business. You see, this whole operation isn't about you or any of the other employees."

That was true of most businesses, Logan thought, but he was surprised to hear the Shareholder admit it so directly. "What would you say it's about?"

"Not what. Who. It's about my son. It's all for him. Once you accept that, you become a functioning part of the team. That's what Level Five folks are."

"And before someone joins Level Five?"

"Prior to that, they're mostly just hanging around, biding time."

"But—and excuse me for overhearing you again—weren't you saying something to your attorney about other employees receiving the whole thing?"

The Shareholder beamed. "Yes. The whole company is for my son. But he wants to share it with everyone on his team. They will all become full inheritors with him."

"Just the people on Level Five?"

"Yes. But you have to remember, everyone on Level Four will one day be on Level Five, as will many from the first three levels."

"But how can they all inherit the whole thing?"

The Shareholder laughed. "That's what I told my lawyer to figure out."

Logan sat quietly for a moment, then took a drink. "So…"

"Yes?"

"I guess I've answered my question about Level Five."

"I guess you have. There's only one more question you have to answer, isn't there?"

Logan returned to the Director's desk. The Director was there; whether he was waiting for him, Logan couldn't tell.

"How was your meeting with the Shareholder?"

"Quite enlightening."

"Did you finish your analysis of Level Five?"

"Yes, definitely."

"Is it what you expected?"

"No, not exactly. It's counterintuitive, like the Share—, like your father said."

The Director smiled. "He always says that." He reached into his desk and retrieved a manila folder. "Your HR file. As I recall, when you started here, I told you you'd have a certain option if you completed your task."

"Yes, I remember."

"Well, you've done a wonderful job on your assignment."

"Thank you. Can I ask you something? Why did you have me tell you about problems you were already aware of?"

"It always helps to have feedback from a fresh set of eyes."

"But nothing I reported was new to you."

"Well, maybe. But it was new to you. Now you know the problems too. Which enables you to make an informed decision about which level you want to work on."

"Yes sir." Logan hesitated. "I guess what I really need to decide is whether I want to work for my own sake or for yours."

"Well…" The Director reached into the file and pulled out an envelope. "No."

"No? I thought that's what Level Five was all about."

"It is. But you can't make that choice now."

"Why not?"

"Because the real issue right now isn't dedicating yourself to working for my purposes. That's the mistake made on Level Four—people think they need to rededicate themselves and then just try harder. But that produces nothing. You don't have it within you to work as I do. Not yet."

"So what's the issue?"

"Level Five is about outlook. That's all you can dedicate yourself to—learning to see as I see. When you see as I see, you will do as I do. And you will produce the true product of this company."

He handed the envelope to Logan. "Take that home and look it over. It's an offer sheet. I can give you a permanent position on any of Levels One through Four—a nice job title with good pay and advancement. Or, if you like, you can accept a position with me as an intern."

"And how long would I be an intern?"

"Always."

"Always? I'd never get promoted?"

"Logan, everyone on Level Five is an intern. They are all life-long learners. They simply learn from me."

Logan looked down and contemplated. The Director sat silently. Finally Logan looked up at him. "Part of me really wants to do that. To be up here with you. To learn from you. But…"

"You have a concern."

"I'm just not exactly sure how that's going to sound—'I'm a permanent intern.'"

"Sound to whom?"

"Well, to someone like my father, I suppose."

"Ah, yes. How has your father reacted to your employment here so far?"

"Pretty well. But he thinks I need to settle down into a real job. I mean, on one of the first four levels."

"I see. I suppose your definition of a real job depends on what you think we are here to accomplish."

The Director leaned forward. "Logan, you're right. You may never please your father by learning from me." He smiled warmly. "But you will please mine."

# About the Author

DAVID GREGORY is the author of *Dinner with a Perfect Stranger: An Invitation Worth Considering* and *A Day with a Perfect Stranger* and the coauthor of two nonfiction books. After a ten-year business career, he returned to school to study religion and communications, earning two master's degrees. David is a native of Texas.

For a downloadable readers' group guide
with questions for reflection and discussion,
go to www.thenextlevelbook.com.

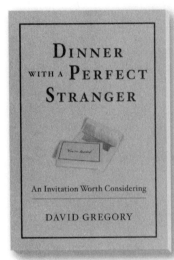

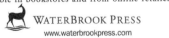

9/09   3495 2041

F  Gregory